MW00915896

ISBN: 978-1-990171-11-6 (eBook)
ISBN: 978-1-990171-10-9 (Paperback)

This book is a work of fiction. Names, characters, and places are products of the author's imagination or are used fictitiously, and any resemblance to actual persons, living or dead, events, business establishments or locales is entirely coincidental.

Cover image by Bobooks.

First edition, 2021.

To everyone who loves living wild!

THE WOLVES OF
ELEMENTA

ROYAL RIVALRY

PROLOGUE

Many moons ago...

Prince Delta woke to the sound of crashing waves. *Huh?* the Water Wolf wondered. His thoughts were fragmented and slow. *Where am I? What happened?* The young prince opened his eyes—then immediately let out a yelp.

Looming over him was a seagull. The bird stared at him with one suspicious, beady eye. Before Prince Delta could scare the seagull away, it gave him a hard peck on the forehead, then glided into the bright blue sky. *Ow,* the Water Wolf thought, rubbing the pain away with a paw.

Black sand squelched beneath Delta's pads as he stood. A ferocious headache immediately seized him. *What is going on here?* the prince wondered frantically. *Where am I?!* The stench of smoke hit his sensitive nose as he looked around the gigantic island. He did not recognize this place. There were black spikes everywhere, along with lava rivers and frequent patches of fire.

And then it came to him.

I think I remember now, the prince thought mournfully. Delta had escaped the Water Pack Empire

1

last night, wanting to get away from all the boring rules that dictated his life. He'd especially wanted to get away from his parents. King Fin and Queen Ripple were the most overbearing wolves someone could imagine. They would lecture their son simply because he wasn't holding a spoon properly. Just the thought of it made Delta clench his teeth.

He was planning to return home eventually, of course, but he had needed a night of freedom to keep himself sane. But how did everything end up going so wrong? Why was he here?

His headache began to worsen. Delta cautiously felt the back of his head with a paw. Dust and fragments of rock fell to the ground at his slight touch. How embarrassing. Delta must have gotten trapped in a powerful current, hitting his head on a boulder in the process, then was washed ashore while unconscious... ending up here—wherever *here* was. It was the only explanation.

Delta scanned the volcanic island again. It was creepy, yet oddly exciting. With a shiver of awe, the prince wondered if he had stumbled across an unexplored land.

I left the empire seeking adventure, Delta thought, *and destiny brought me here. Maybe I should explore this island for a bit. I've already been gone from my empire for so long. What's the harm in staying away for just a little longer?* The Water Wolf hesitated, shifting his weight from paw to paw. *If my parents caught me exploring, they'd be furious.* He grinned. *But they aren't here right now.*

Delta lifted his head. He strode confidently to the heart of the island. The sand gave way to hard volcanic rocks as he reached the end of the beach. Black spikes surrounded him on all sides, sticking out of the ground like glistening fangs. Smoke billowed through the sky, rancid and terrible.

The Water Wolf was seized by a loud coughing fit. Instantly the silence of the black hills and lava pools was shattered. Delta froze, hoping that he hadn't alerted anything, or anyone, of his presence. When all remained silent and still, the prince continued exploring.

He quickly got the feeling that he wasn't alone. Delta inhaled, trying to take in all the nearby scents, but his nose was assaulted by the rancid tang of smoke. If there was indeed someone watching him, he wouldn't be able to tell, unless he heard or saw the stalker. Delta gulped, feeling suddenly worried. His ears flattened.

Maybe I should have stopped to think before wandering into unknown territory, the prince thought. *Lava pools? Volcanic rocks? Clouds of smoke? This must be Fire Wolf land. Or the outskirts of it at least.*

Delta paused. *I should turn back,* he thought. *This isn't worth running into an angry Fire Wolf. I just hope it's not already too late to get out of here alive.* The prince turned around. He padded to the ocean, his pawsteps silent and deliberate. *Slow and steady. I'm almost at the beach. Once I get out of this maze of spikes, I'll run the rest of the way to the ocean, and then I'll be safely beneath the waves.*

Without warning, black pebbles skidded down the slanted spike behind him. Delta whipped around with wide eyes. Before he could run, a Fire Wolf leapt forward, tumbling into the Water Wolf and squashing him beneath her.

Delta cowered underneath the stranger. He'd never been in a fight before! He was a *prince*, not a guard. He covered his eyes with his paws, trembling, hoping for the stranger's mercy. He expected a menacing growl, but instead heard an embarrassed yelp. "Oops! I'm so sorry," the Fire Wolf said. "I meant to land beside you and look really cool. That, uh, failed miserably, didn't it?"

Delta slowly moved his paws away. He looked up at the Fire Wolf in astonishment. She was... beautiful. Her bright yellow eyes were warm, and her light red fur reminded Delta of a sunrise. When she smiled at him, his heart began to flutter strangely. Why was his heart fluttering? This had never happened before.

When the Fire Wolf reached out a paw to help him stand, Delta surprised himself by taking it. After rising off the ground, he merely blinked at the Fire Wolf, unsure of what else to do. "Hi," she said cheerfully. "I'm Ash. It's nice to meet you."

Delta took a step back and shook his head, snapping out of his trance. "I beg your pardon," he protested. "It's nice to meet *me*? Are you blind? I'm a Water Wolf. You know, the sworn enemy and opposite of your pack? You should be tearing off my fur, not greeting me. Why in Elementa are you being nice to me?" Delta began to wonder if Ash was out of her mind... or just special. His brain told him to flee into the ocean, while his heart wanted to get to know her. *What is wrong with me?* the prince scolded himself. *If my parents ever found out about this, they'd lecture me for days, then have my head!*

"Why not?" Ash responded with another warm smile. "I've always thought the rules separating the packs are dumb. Why should we hate one another just because we're different? I think the other elementals are cool. Especially Water Wolves!" She lifted to full height so she could gaze at his tail and fins. "Wow! You're pretty fishy. Not fishy, as in suspicious. Fishy, as in, you look like a fish! Is your name Fish?"

Delta was smiling without realizing it. "My name is Delta," he said. "Prince Delta of the Water Pack

5

Empire." Oh geez. Why was he trying to impress her? Was his fluttery heart the one to blame for this? Delta tried to push away his affection for Ash, tried to think sensibly about talking with his sworn enemy, but he couldn't. There was just something about this Fire Wolf that made him feel alive and free.

"A prince!" Ash exclaimed. "Wow! This is like a fairy tale I heard as a pup. Wouldn't it be funny if I fell in love with you? Oh! But you don't think this is one of those tragic love stories, do you? The kind where one of us dies in the end? Do you think I'll be the one to die, or you? Or both? Ack!"

Delta coughed. "First of all, we just met," he spluttered. "Secondly, I can't die now. I have too much to do. There's definitely no time to die. My busy schedule just won't allow for it." Delta kept his face serious for a moment, then gave her a bright smile. "Just kidding."

Ash laughed—*genuinely laughed*. None of the noble wolves in the Water Pack Empire ever laughed at Delta's jokes. Listening to Ash chuckle was almost hard to process after so many years of disregard. If this was a dream, the prince hoped that he wouldn't wake up soon.

Once the slender Fire Wolf stopped laughing, she flicked her ear in amusement. "Fishy and funny?" Ash said with a grin. "A perfect combo. You're way more interesting than any Fire Wolf I've ever met." She laughed nervously. "But if any of my packmates ever saw us together, we'd both be in a whole lot of trouble. It's a good thing nobody lives on this part of the island but me."

"You're all alone?" the Water Wolf asked in a small voice. Ash hadn't sounded bothered by that, but Delta couldn't help but feel sad for her. Surely it was better to have pushy family than to have no family at all. Living alone seemed dreadful.

"It's no big deal," Ash responded genuinely. "My brother comes to visit me all the time." She suddenly halted with wide eyes. "Oh, of all the times to be forgetful! Back, back, back!" Ash hurriedly escorted him toward the ocean. "You need to hide. *Now*. Flame is here. I can't believe I forgot about that. Argh! I'm such a scatterbrain."

As if on cue, the sound of pawsteps emerged from the silence as Flame approached. "Ash?" he called in his slow, monotonous voice. "Ash, is that you? What's going on over there? Who are you talking to? Is everything okay?"

Ash frantically paced along the shore as Delta scrambled into the ocean. His instincts screamed for him to swim far away from the Fire Pack and never return, but instead he halted and gazed at Ash, only his head above the surface.

"Okay, uh, hide here," she nervously told the Water Wolf. "I'll take care of him." Ash turned around and tried to look natural. Delta dipped his head beneath the waves, keeping only his ears out of the water. He listened.

"Hi, Flame!" Ash greeted with a bit too much enthusiasm. "I was just, uh, talking to myself. You know how I am. Ha ha. I'm *such* a weird-o." Delta could only imagine the awkward smile on her face. Poor Ash. He hoped that she wouldn't get in trouble because of him.

"Uh huh," Flame responded slowly. There was a pause. "Why do I smell Water Wolf?"

There was a crunching sound as Ash gripped the sand with her paws. "A seagull must have flown here after visiting Water Pack territory," she said, desperately trying to keep her voice steady. "No biggie."

"All right," Flame yawned. "If those seagulls return, let me know. I don't want them stinking up the beach with any more Water Wolf scents. Until then... I'm going to nap. See you later." His pawsteps faded with distance, until Delta could hear them no more. Flame was gone. However, the prince remained hidden until Ash splashed her paw in the water, signalling that it was safe for him to come out. Delta lifted his head out of the water as he paddled to shore.

"Phew!" Ash said, her eyes wide. "That was close! I thought we were going to get caught for sure!" Her smile dropped. "I can't believe I forgot about Flame. If he wasn't visiting, I could have shown you around my beach. But you can't stay here. It's too risky."

Delta opened and closed his mouth a few times, at a loss for words. He had to leave? Now? He had just been getting to know Ash! The thought of leaving her forever made his heart twist with grief.

"I guess this is goodbye, then," Ash said sullenly. Her tail drooped and her ears flattened. "Our love story ended a lot quicker than I thought it would." She gave him a sad smile. "Oh well. Not everything has a fairy tale ending. I'm just glad we got to meet in the first place. And besides. You're a prince. I'm nobody special. It wasn't going to work out anyway."

Delta lifted out of the water. He placed his paw on hers, looking into her eyes. "We'll make it work," he blurted. "I don't want this to be the end of our story. I know this sounds really sappy, but I think you're my destiny—my other half. I don't care about my royal status. The only thing I care about is you." He blushed and looked away. What was he talking about?! He'd only just met Ash... and yet he already knew how much she meant to him.

Ash looked surprised that a wolf cared about her so much. "Maybe we can meet again," she said. "I know it's dangerous and stupid, especially for you, but it might just work. Flame is only visiting for the rest of this moon cycle, and after that, it'll just be me again. We can see each other as often as we want. The two of us don't have to be alone anymore."

Delta grinned. "Can I say something really cheesy?" he asked.

Ash nodded. "Go on," she said.

"I just have this feeling," Delta said, "that you and I are going to change the world."

***

Rain pattered outside the beachside den, drumming against the black sand. Ash and Delta were curled together, their tails intertwined. Ash slept peacefully, her soft snores joining the rhythmic raindrops. But Delta couldn't sleep.

He watched the storm outside without moving, his ears perked and eyes wide. Something felt wrong. He could feel in his heart that some terrible event was coming their way. And once it struck, nothing would ever be the same again.

Delta flinched when thunder rolled through the sky, ominous and fierce.

It had been many moons since the wolves first met. Since that fateful day, Delta had been struggling to balance being a prince, and being a partner to Ash. He sometimes went nights without sleep, swimming across the ocean and back to live two separate lives. When Delta did manage to doze off, it was during his parents' lectures, or horribly boring lessons with his tutors. It didn't take long for the nobles to realize that something was wrong with their prince. Thankfully, they hadn't managed to discover the reason for his absent-mindedness yet. Or, at least, that's what Delta hoped.

Although he constantly felt nervous about being discovered, he'd never felt as worried as he did now. He peered out at the violent ocean, his emotions as tumultuous as the white capped waves. Delta suddenly froze. When lightning flickered across the sky, it lit up everything, including the shark-like fins of Water Wolves that sliced across the water. It was an army of Water Wolves—and they were approaching rapidly.

Delta frantically shook Ash awake. She lifted her head and looked at him, understanding immediately. The fear in her mate's eyes said it all: they had been discovered at last. "I'll get Nautilus," Ash said shakily. She rose to her paws and hurried to the back of the den, where their pup dozed.

"Nautilus," she whispered, prodding him urgently. "Nautilus, wake up. We have to go." Ash looked like she wanted to carry him away by the scruff, but he was too big for that now. They'd have to flee by paw.

Nautilus lifted his head, blinking at his parents with wide green eyes. He was in his Water Wolf form, like usual. The pup had quickly learned that his Fire Wolf form meant danger and singed fur. "Go?" he asked meekly. "Go where, Mommy?"

Delta clenched his teeth. The poor pup was barely old enough to speak, and already danger had found him. It wasn't fair. Nautilus was a good pup. He was kind and loveable and understanding. But he didn't belong in a divided world like Elementa. If only the pup had been born during a time of peace among the packs. Things would have been a lot simpler.

Ash looked like she was trying hard not to cry. "Someplace far away," she responded. "Everything is going to be all right. Do you understand? Mommy and Daddy are going to take care of you. Come with me. Make sure you're very quiet."

Nautilus followed Ash to the edge of the cave, fumbling slightly on his webbed paws. The pup halted near the exit, blinking up at his father. "What about Daddy?" he asked Ash. "Why isn't he coming with us?" Even though Nautilus was still so young, he could perceive emotions so well. All it took was one look at Delta to realize how bad their situation was.

Delta gave his son an affectionate lick. "I have to stay here to protect you," he responded. Delta wished there was time to explain, but Nautilus seemed to understand. The tiny pup walked into the rain, following his mother along the beach. Mother and son broke into a sprint, their paws kicking up loose clumps of sand. Delta watched them go while holding his breath. Would they manage to escape in time?

Without warning, dark shapes rose out of the ocean. Delta turned to face them. He bared his teeth and growled. Despite his fierce appearance, he felt an explosion of fear. Leading the army was Queen Ripple and King Fin—Delta's own parents. They wielded tridents and wore thick armour. Clearly, they hadn't come here for a friendly visit.

The royals locked gazes for what felt like an eternity. Queen Ripple's eyes eventually slunk over to Ash and Nautilus as they darted across the beach. "Get them," she ordered the guards. "Bring them to me alive for now. As for my son. Seize him."

Delta was pounced on. He was dragged to the ground and squashed against the black sand. With wide eyes, he watched helplessly as Ash and Nautilus became surrounded. They were herded back to the king and queen, eyes bright with fear. Ash kept her pup close, ready to die to protect him. She bared her fangs and growled boldly at Delta's parents. However, the king and queen couldn't care less about the Fire Wolf. Their attention was fully on Nautilus.

"So the reports we heard are true," King Fin mused, not once taking his eyes off his grandson. "We really do have a new addition to the family. He looks like a fine young wolf. Strong. Healthy. Smart. It's a shame, though, that he's tainted with Fire Wolf blood."

Delta's paws began to tremble. Where was his father going with this?

Nautilus abruptly sneezed. He changed into a Fire Wolf involuntarily, his paws glowing red with heat. The sand below him sizzled. Surprised murmurs rippled through the crowd. Some guards even took a step back, as if they were frightened by the hybrid. Nobody had seen anything like Nautilus for hundreds, maybe thousands, of years.

Queen Ripple narrowed her eyes. She glared at her grandson for a long moment, then looked at Delta. "You've brought shame to us all," she hissed lividly. "This pup is an abomination. You were a fool to have any relationship outside the pack. If only there were more heirs to the throne. I would dispose of you here and now, Prince Delta." The queen nodded at the guards seizing her son. "Release him."

Delta stood slowly, raindrops sliding down his muzzle. His gills fluttered nervously as he faced his furious parents. This was a living nightmare.

"We will present you with two decisions," King Fin said in his most diplomatic voice. "The choice you make is entirely yours. You may either stay loyal to your new family and perish alongside them. Or, you may come with us quietly, never speak of this again, and leave this wretched island behind forever. We will spare the Fire Wolf and pup if you agree to turn your back on them forever."

Delta peeled his gaze away from his parents, turning his head to look pleadingly at Ash. She gave him a slow nod, understanding in her eyes. They both knew that this was the last time they'd ever see each other again. Although this choice was the most difficult one to make, it was also the most obvious.

"Fine," he choked out. "Just... please leave them alone. I'm the one to blame for all this. Ash and Nautilus are good wolves." Delta wished he could plead with his parents, to find some other way, but he knew that it would be a waste of breath. There was no reasoning with the king and queen once they'd made up their minds. At least they were offering mercy in the first place.

The world spun beneath Delta's paws as he stumbled to the ocean, one parent flanking him on each side. Once the water was up to his shoulders, Delta turned to meet Nautilus' eyes.

He was so tiny. So young and helpless. Although Delta would miss Ash terribly, it was their pup that worried him the most. How was an outcast like him supposed to survive in this hostile world? *At least he has Ash to protect him,* the prince thought with a violent shudder. It felt like he was being torn in half. *With her by his side, he'll survive.*

Delta hesitated a moment longer, looking into the eyes of Nautilus. He then forced himself to dive beneath the waves, ears ringing. He followed his parents to the Water Pack Empire in a daze, leaving everything he'd ever loved behind.

Although the worst had happened, Delta refused to let go of hope. Even after ascending to kingship moons later, he still tried to remain positive, even if his guards could find no trace of Ash or Nautilus. Life was full of unexpected surprises, after all. Good things always came to those who waited. And so Delta was patient. He knew in his heart that one day soon—very soon—he would see his family again.

CHAPTER 1

Today...

"I have a bad feeling about this," Nautilus whimpered. "This is going to end badly. I just know it." Nautilus anxiously fiddled with the fins on his tail. "Can I go home?"

Aurora dipped her wing in the ocean, then playfully splashed Nautilus. "You are going home," she said happily.

Nautilus frowned. "I meant my den," he replied. "Not some deep, dark, scary ocean that I've never been in before. It's probably full of wolves who hate me."

Aurora gave Nautilus a friendly bump on the side. "Nobody hates you, Nautilus," she told him. "You're awesome! I bet the Water Wolves will love you."

Nautilus timidly stared at the ocean. He kept silent, as if hoping Aurora would miraculously forget he existed, and leave him alone.

"Just think of how exciting this is, Nautilus," Aurora immediately continued, in her overly optimistic voice. "You'll meet so many Water Wolves. You'll finally see the underwater kingdom. Maybe you'll even find your Water Wolf parent. Aren't you looking forward to that?"

Nautilus stared down at his webbed paws. A salty breeze flowed through his dark blue fur, while waves crashed on the island shore in front of him. *Looking forward to meeting my Water Wolf parent?* Nautilus thought. *Not really. Both of my parents are strangers to me. I don't remember them.*

That was why he'd avoided the Fire Pack and Water Pack territories all his life. The thought of running into his parents—the parents who had abandoned him as a pup—made Nautilus shudder.

"Uh, sure," Nautilus lied. "That would be cool, I guess."

"Let's not lose sight of our mission," Ember commented from behind them. He sat underneath the shade of a palm tree, his orange eyes shining in the shadows. "We're here to convince the Water Pack to unite with the rest of Elementa."

"Easier said than done," Nautilus mumbled.

Aurora shrugged. "I think we can do it," she announced. "After all, we managed to bring peace to the Sky Pack. If we can defeat Queen Tempest *and* change the minds of all those Sky Wolves, I don't see why we can't unify with the Water Pack."

Nautilus looked away from his friends. *How can they be so confident?* he asked himself. *They're acting like this is going to be some easy, simple task. They're so sure that all of Elementa can be united. Aren't they afraid of failure? I know I am.*

Nautilus felt queasy. *Maybe they're so calm because they aren't taking the lead this time,* he thought. Nautilus clutched the sand with his claws. *This mission has fallen onto my shoulders. Now it's my turn to be a hero. But if I fail, everything will be my fault.* The thought made him feel dizzy.

"Um, guys?" Nautilus asked Aurora and Ember. "I was just wondering if I *really* need to go to the Water Pack? Why don't we find Sandstorm, and try unifying with the Earth Pack instead? That wouldn't be so bad, would it?" Nautilus' gills fluttered anxiously. "Just think about it. In the Water Pack, I'll be on my own, since you two can't swim. You guys know how clumsy I am. I'll mess this up for sure. We better play it safe and go to the Earth Pack. Right?"

Ember flattened his ears. His dark red fur flowed in the ocean breeze. "You aren't thinking of backing out of this, are you?" he asked in a low voice. "Because it's much too late for that. I've already swam all the way to this island, and I'm not letting it be for nothing. You're going to the Water Pack whether you like it or not, Nautilus."

Well. That settles it, then.

Nautilus, Aurora, and Ember had decided to use this island as their base, while they spent their time bringing peace to the Water Pack. It wasn't that big, but it was cozy, and had all they needed to survive. There were coconuts, fish that swam in the pond of fresh rain water, and plenty of palm trees for shelter. It wasn't half bad, if you asked Nautilus. If only he could stay up here, instead of exploring the dark ocean below. He was not looking forward to meeting other Water Wolves.

It was strange, though, that not every Water Wolf lived in the underwater kingdom. There were more islands not too far away from here. When Aurora had flown over them to explore, she had found a few Water Wolves living on them. Aurora had described the wolves as looking sad and homesick, and constantly staring at the ocean. They looked like prisoners, except there were no cages or chains preventing them from fleeing their islands.

Ember had suggested that the Water Wolves were in some type of banishment from the ocean, but he wasn't entirely sure.

"Can we name our island?" Aurora suddenly suggested. "I think that would be cute, don't you?" She enthusiastically ruffled the feathers on her wings, smiling brightly. Although Aurora carried a long, somewhat intimidating scar on her snout from the fight with Sandstorm, she was nothing but a warm ray of sunshine.

Ember's expression softened immediately. He always lost his grumpiness whenever he looked at Aurora, which was... suspicious.

Does Ember like her? Nautilus wondered. *And does Aurora like him back? If they're in love, would that make me a third wheel?*

Ember gave Aurora a smile, making Nautilus shudder. Happiness and Ember were a strange combination, to say the least. "I think that's a fun idea," Ember replied. "Do you have anything in mind?" If Nautilus had suggested naming the island, Ember probably would have clawed him.

Aurora paused thoughtfully. "How about... Ember Island?" she asked. "A great island named after an even greater wolf. What do you think?"

"I think Aurora Island is better," Ember replied happily.

Aurora sat beside Ember and wrapped a wing around him. "Okay, how about a compromise?" she said. "Let's name this place Emora Island. It's a combination of both our names."

Ember looked like the happiest wolf in the world. "I love it."

Gross! So they are in love! Nautilus thought with a shudder. *Okay, now I'm definitely a third wheel. I guess I have a fourth elemental power after all—invisibility. They're acting like I'm not even here.* He frowned. *If only Sandstorm were here. Then I wouldn't have to be stuck with Aurora and Ember's sappy shenanigans.* Nautilus flattened his ears. *And besides, Nautilus Island is obviously the best name.*

He decided to use his friends' distraction as an opportunity. *Maybe if I hide for long enough, they'll forget all about my mission in the Water Pack, and decide to go to the Earth Pack instead.* Nautilus smiled nervously. *Then they can dump my responsibilities on Sandstorm, and I'll be able to relax again. Fighting a vicious queen was hard work, after all. I deserve some time to rest!*

Before Nautilus could even take a step, Ember glared at him. "Where do you think you're going?" the Fire Wolf demanded, back to his grumpy self.

Nautilus yelped. "Um, nowhere!" he replied. "Well, except to the Water Pack, of course. Because that's where my big heroic destiny is. I just love being a hero. Why *wouldn't* I want to go into the ocean? Hooray for daring missions!"

Aurora walked toward Nautilus, giving him a reassuring smile. "You'll be great, Nautilus," she told him kindly. "Don't feel like you have to rush into this. Why don't you take things slow? Get to know the Water Pack first, and try to meet some friends. You don't need to go marching up to the royal castle, demanding that the Water Pack immediately unite with the rest of Elementa."

Nautilus flicked his tail. "Oh, really?" he asked sarcastically. "Because that was my plan all along."

"Har har, very funny," Aurora replied. "Anyway, I know that you'll be amazing, Nautilus. Ember and I trust you. Maybe it's time you start trusting yourself."

Nautilus turned around before they could see his embarrassed expression. Was Nautilus' lack of self-trust so obvious? Could they really see how little confidence he had? Nautilus was sure he had hidden his self-esteem issues better. How humiliating! Aurora and Ember must think he feared his own shadow—which Nautilus didn't, just for the record. Nautilus had stopped being afraid of his own shadow moons ago.

"I better go," Nautilus mumbled. He'd rather be at the bottom of the ocean than be embarrassed like this. Without looking back, or saying another word, Nautilus dragged himself toward the beach. *Would my friends notice if I swam right back to my cave on the beach, instead of going to the Water Pack?* he wondered. *Would they care if I never came back?*

"Good luck, Nautilus!" Aurora cheered from behind him. "You're going to do great!"

"Yeah, uh, you got this," Ember added in a reluctant voice, as if Aurora had forced him to say something. "Don't get eaten by a shark, okay?"

They will care if I don't come back, Nautilus realized. He paused near the shore, releasing a gusty sigh. *Whether I like it or not, I have friends now. Friends who are counting on me. I won't let them down. Not after all the support they've given me.*

Nautilus slowly waded into the light blue waves, walking deeper into the ocean until the water reached his neck. Nautilus closed his eyes for a moment, trying to control his racing heart. Then, after releasing a deep breath, Nautilus plunged his head beneath the water.

There was no going back now. This was only the beginning of Nautilus' journey... and the start of a destiny that would shake Elementa to its core. Nautilus didn't realize it, but in this moment, he had launched the beginning of the end.

Nothing was ever going to be the same again.

CHAPTER 2

Nautilus officially hated the ocean. The salt water stung his eyes and irritated his gills. He struggled to swim in the powerful, chaotic current. There were strange, vibrant fish everywhere. It was all so foreign to him. Nautilus had never experienced anything like this before. It was as if he had dived right into another world. A world in which he didn't belong.

This is nothing like the lagoons back home, Nautilus thought wistfully. *It was so peaceful at my den. Oh, I wish I could go back. Why did destiny choose to give me a daring mission? I'm the least heroic wolf in all of Elementa, for the moon's sake!*

An underwater wave suddenly zoomed through the ocean. Nautilus yelped as he got stuck in its pull. He was sent tumbling backward. Nautilus thrashed helplessly, feeling like a dismal piece of driftwood. Luckily, he crashed into a tall branch of coral, and managed to regain control.

Nautilus paused for a long moment, his gills fluttering while he caught his breath. Then, Nautilus gingerly swam forward. He immediately tumbled back as another wave rolled by. Nautilus nervously gripped the coral with his claws, using it to anchor himself.

This is hopeless! Nautilus thought. *I should go back to Emora Island and tell my friends the truth. I'm not a wolf they can count on. I'm too much of a coward, too much of a klutz, too slow to figure things out, and too afraid to take action.* Nautilus' eyes began to sting, and he wondered if it was possible to cry underwater. *Maybe Aurora and Ember would be better off without me. Since the beginning, I've just been slowing them down. Maybe it's time to go our separate ways, and for me to stop holding them back.*

Nautilus let out a sigh. A tiny stream of bubbles was launched out of his nose. *No, I can't disappoint them,* Nautilus reminded himself. *Even if I am less heroic than Aurora and Ember, I can still do my best. If I give up right away, I'll certainly be the failure I fear of becoming. I owe my friends a good effort.*

Nautilus closed his eyes. *Just think about what Sandstorm would do,* he told himself. *Sandstorm is everything I'd like to be. She's brave, confident, a quick thinker, and always ready for a challenge. Would it be a dumb idea to try imagining myself as her? It's worth a shot, I guess. I just hope Sandstorm never finds out about this. She'll probably claw me or something.*

Nautilus let out a long breath, then opened his eyes. *Grr, I'm Sandstorm, and I'm afraid of nothing! I'm so awesome. Even the ocean fears me!* Nautilus boldly swam forward, propelling himself through the water with powerful strokes. *Get out of my way, ocean. I'm swimming here! If you mess with me, I'll find a way to bite you, even if you are just water. Ha! I'm the coolest.*

Nautilus felt like a fool for acting so silly, but in all honesty, impersonating Sandstorm gave him a boost of confidence. It was fun, pretending to be a wolf that inspired him. Nautilus began to feel less afraid as he swam through the unknown.

Keep moving, sea turtle, Nautilus thought cockily. *You don't want to cross paths with me. I'm the fiercest thing in this reef.* Nautilus smiled. *What are you looking at, sea horse? Hey, eel! You aren't planning to mess with me, are you? Yeah, you better camouflage, octopus!*

Nautilus suddenly froze. Wait a minute. Why *was* that octopus camouflaging? Didn't they do that when they felt threatened or unsafe? That octopus couldn't possibly be afraid of Nautilus, could it? Had it sensed his new headstrong attitude and decided to hide? No. That couldn't be it.

Something was wrong.

Nautilus immediately began to panic. *I need to hide,* he thought. *There's some type of danger that I'm not seeing. I should hurry. Hurry, Nautilus. Hurry. Find shelter. Find someplace to hide. Go. Go!* Nautilus forced himself to remain still, instead of scurrying under a rock to hide for all eternity. *I need to get a grip. I'm probably just overreacting, like normal. I'm not a scaredy wolf anymore. I'm Sandstorm, the bravest and best wolf ever. No more hiding. It's time I start facing my problems, instead of running away from them. Whatever scared the octopus is far less scary than me. Right...?*

Nautilus nervously looked around. He couldn't see anything that seemed like a threat. In fact, the reef had grown significantly empty in the last couple of seconds. *No creatures, no danger,* Nautilus thought, trying to reassure himself. *I'm sure everything is completely fine. This is normal... I hope.*

Still, Nautilus couldn't help but look over his shoulder every few seconds, while he slowly continued to swim.

There was a large forest of kelp up ahead. Nautilus hesitated by its edge, thinking of all the ways something could go wrong in there. *Sandstorm wouldn't be worried about the leaves strangling her,* Nautilus thought with a frown. *I shouldn't be worried, either. Who's ever heard of a wolf getting strangled by some leaves? Not me, that's for sure.*

Nautilus swam closer to the kelp forest, then paused, right before he swam inside. *Wait. What if there's something scary in there? Maybe I should just swim around this place to be safe.*

Nautilus hesitated yet again. *Aurora and Ember would have been halfway through the kelp forest by now,* he realized. *They wouldn't have gone around it.*

Nautilus let out a frustrated sigh. *For Elementa's sake, Nautilus, make a decision!* he snapped at himself. *Sandstorm, Aurora, and Ember would have gone through the kelp forest. I'll be brave like them. I'm going in, and that's final.* Nautilus lashed his fish-like tail, then plunged into the dark green depths.

Kelp and seaweed uncomfortably slid over his fur as he swam. Plants obscured Nautilus' vision on all sides. It was almost impossible to see even a few tail lengths ahead. *Please don't let there be a sea monster in here,* Nautilus thought anxiously. *Please let me be the biggest thing swimming in this place. Please don't—Ack!*

Nautilus was abruptly yanked backward. He screamed, producing an explosion of bubbles. *Sea monster!* Nautilus thought. *It's got me! Ah!* It took a few moments of thrashing and shrieking to realize that a creature *hadn't* ensnared him. Nautilus' tail had gotten tangled up by some strands of kelp.

How embarrassing!

Nautilus sheepishly twisted around so he faced his tail. The tangle was worse than Nautilus had expected. He pulled his tail with full force, trying to free himself. It was no use. *You've got to be kidding me,* Nautilus thought. *Oh well. This could've been worse. I'd rather free myself from kelp, than from the jaws of some monster.* Nautilus hooked a claw around a strand of kelp, then began to unravel himself.

Without warning, there was a rush of cold water. It felt like a gust of wind, reminding him of the gales Aurora produced whenever she flew overhead.

Nautilus froze. His gaze wildly darted around, trying to locate the source of the ominous current. All Nautilus could see was seaweed, seaweed, and more seaweed. Fear and frustration pumped through his veins. Nautilus returned his attention to his tail, untangling himself with as much speed as possible. This was very bad. He was as hopeless as a fish in a net right now!

There was another burst of water. A dark shadow abruptly fell over Nautilus, then vanished as quickly as it had appeared. *Something is hunting me,* Nautilus realized, horror-struck. *I need to get out of here now!* He hurriedly sunk his fangs into the thick kelp, trying to shred it off his tail.

After what felt like forever, Nautilus managed to free himself. There was no time to celebrate.

A gigantic creature immediately darted forward. Rows upon rows of jagged teeth zoomed toward Nautilus. SHARK!

Nautilus threw himself out of the way. The shark missed him by a paw's length. Nautilus whipped around and swam as fast as his stubby paws allowed. Kelp smacked against his face. Fear thundered through his veins. Nautilus could hear the shark gliding through the water behind him—it was catching up fast. Was this the end for Nautilus?

He suddenly broke through the kelp forest, reaching its end. What he saw on the other side terrified him more than the shark. There was a group of Water Wolves swimming in the distance, armed with sharp, battle-ready tridents. Beyond the wolves was none other than the Water Pack Empire.

Before Nautilus could even scream for help, the group of Water Wolves noticed him and the shark as they rapidly approached. Then... the Water Wolves laughed. Nautilus was so startled by their reaction that he nearly fainted. What in Elementa was wrong with them? Did they *want* to see him get eaten alive?!

The shark put on a sudden burst of speed. As fast as lightning, it caught Nautilus' leg in its jaw. Nautilus let out a rather undignified squeal of fear, knowing that his doom had arrived at long last. Torn to bits by a shark. How could fate be so cruel?

"Hey, calm down," said an unusually clear voice. Was Nautilus hallucinating? Wolves couldn't talk underwater... could they? It certainly wasn't the shark speaking. At least, Nautilus desperately hoped that it wasn't. That would be horrifying and wrong on so many levels. "She only wants to play with you. Why are you screaming?"

Nautilus hadn't realized until now that he had slammed his eyes shut. He hesitated for a long moment, then slowly blinked open his eyes. Embarrassment crashed down on him with more force than a tsunami.

The group of Water Wolves were staring at him. Some were still laughing at him. All while he was stuck between the fangs of a shark. Was this some kind of messed up nightmare?

One of the Water Wolves gently patted the shark with his paw. "Let him go," he told it. To Nautilus' absolute bewilderment, the shark obeyed. The creature spat Nautilus out, as if he was nothing more than a chew toy. Was this monstrosity the Water Wolves' pet?!

Nautilus scrambled backward, his green eyes wider than a full moon. His heart rapidly slammed inside his chest. Nautilus' dark blue fur bristled.

"What's the matter with you?" another Water Wolf asked, not unkindly, but not gently, either. "What are you so freaked out about? Haven't you seen a shark before?"

Nautilus hesitated for a long moment, then shook his head. *Never that close before,* he thought with a shudder.

A large, sea green Water Wolf leaned forward. She studied Nautilus like he was some type of strange seashell. "Can't you talk?" she barked.

Nautilus opened and closed his mouth a few times, feeling rattled. He'd had no idea that Water Wolves could speak underwater. Nautilus had never even attempted trying something so strange before, in all his years of isolation. It didn't seem natural to him.

"Gwrmph," Nautilus said, attempting to say 'no'. He accidentally sucked in a mouthful of salt water. Nautilus coughed and spluttered, producing a frenzy of bubbles that swarmed around the Water Wolves' faces. The sea green wolf waved away the bubbles with her webbed paw, looking less than impressed.

"Maybe there's something wrong with him," someone suggested. He had tentacles instead of arms, and piercing yellow eyes that suspiciously stared at Nautilus.

"Do you think he's lost?" another wolf chimed in. She had a strange antenna on her head. It connected with a glowing orb. "I've never seen him before. Maybe he's a runaway from the Outer Islands. Should we report him to King Delta?"

"Probably," said a wolf with pincers instead of paws.

Nautilus felt an explosion of fear as the Water Wolves loomed closer. They were going to take him to the Water Pack king, whether he liked it or not! *I need to get out of here.* Nautilus whirled around and swam away at full speed. He plunged into the kelp forest, desperate to escape this nightmare.

Nautilus didn't stop swimming until he was certain the Water Wolves weren't following. He gasped and wheezed, trying to catch his breath. Then, Nautilus slowly sunk to the ocean floor, landing on the sand with a soft thump. He wrapped his paws over his face, wanting to block out the entire world.

Nautilus' first encounter with the Water Pack had been an absolute failure. If he couldn't even speak underwater, how was he supposed to unite the entire kingdom with the rest of Elementa? Perhaps Nautilus' mission was doomed to fail, before it even truly begun.

Aurora and Ember had picked the wrong wolf for this job.

CHAPTER 3

Nautilus dragged himself to the shore of Emora Island, feeling miserable and exhausted. Wet sand squelched beneath his paws as he stumbled to dry land. His dark blue fur was soaked with salt water, making him feel uncomfortable in the warm sun. Nautilus shook his pelt, then sauntered away from the beach. He walked further into the island before sitting underneath the shade of a palm tree. A gentle breeze flowed around him.

Nautilus slowly sat down and stared at the ground. The rhythmic sound of crashing waves filled the silence. He turned to face the ocean's direction. Nautilus stared at the sea without moving for a long, long moment. He let out a heavy sigh. *How could I have messed things up so badly?* Nautilus wondered. He felt a sudden surge of anger with himself. *My friends were counting on me to be great. Instead, I became a shark's chew toy, and embarrassed myself in front of a group of Water Wolves.* Nautilus wanted to scream.

I was so lost in that moment. I couldn't even speak—literally. How am I supposed to save the world when I can't even communicate with the Water

Wolves? Nobody will take me seriously. I ruined my only chance at a good first impression. I'm hopeless.

Nautilus hesitated, then changed into his Fire Wolf form. His fish-like tail, webbed paws, and dark blue fur vanished within seconds. Now, his fur was light red, and his paws were so hot that they glowed. Nautilus held up one of his paws and studied it with a frown.

How can I ever truly belong with the Water Wolves when I'm only half of one? Nautilus wondered miserably. *I'll never be a full Water Wolf. Should I even bother trying to be someone I'm not?* Nautilus lowered his paw. He flattened his ears and moved his tail closer to his body. *Perhaps it's time to move on from the Water Pack, and to be a lone wolf again.*

Nautilus returned his gaze to the ocean. There was something about the sea that filled him with energy. Filled him with hope. Filled him with a sense of purpose. Although Nautilus couldn't understand why, he knew that the ocean was calling him. *More like ordering me to go back in,* he thought unhappily. *The ocean sure is giving me a bossy vibe right about now. Guess what, ocean? Maybe I don't want to return to you. You can call me all you want, but it doesn't mean I'm going to answer you. I choose my own destiny, and I choose to go take a nap!*

Nautilus gripped the ground with his claws. *First, I'll have to explain what happened to my friends,* he realized. *I hope they're in a patient mood today.* A rancid smell began to fill the air. Nautilus gasped, realizing that his burning paws had turned the sand black. He immediately transformed back into a harmless Water Wolf, feeling embarrassed.

Nautilus avoided looking at the ocean as he rose to his paws. "Aurora? Ember? Guys?" he called. "I'm back! Um. Where are you?"

No response. All Nautilus could hear was the crashing of waves.

He shrugged. *I'm sure they haven't gone far,* he realized. *They must have moved further along the beach.* Nautilus began to make his way along the outskirts of the island, leaving a trail of pawprints in the sand. As he walked in silence, the sun began to set behind the churning waves. The sky turned light yellow, while the fluffy clouds became a beautiful shade of pink.

Eventually, Nautilus reached the start of his trail of pawprints. He had completely circled the island, and there had been no trace of Aurora or Ember. Nautilus instantly felt nervous. *Has something bad happened?* he wondered.

As if on cue, Nautilus heard the faint, faraway sound of laughter. It was barely audible in the rolling waves and whispering breeze. Nautilus nearly fainted from relief. Aurora and Ember were still here... and having a great time, by the sound of it.

The laughter had come from the middle of the island, inside the miniature jungle. Nautilus was surprised that his friends had ventured in so soon. He wouldn't have been brave enough to explore the depths of Emora Island yet. What if there were creepy bugs lurking around? Nautilus shuddered.

He crept toward the edge of the trees, halting just outside of the jungle's border. *Aurora and Ember were laughing, not shrieking,* he told himself. *They're perfectly fine, and probably aren't getting eaten alive by some freakish spider. For the love of Elementa, Nautilus, stop being afraid of everything! Go meet your friends and stop worrying about every little thing in your life.*

Nautilus pushed past the veil of leaves. It was surprisingly beautiful inside. Palm trees swayed serenely in the breeze. A tiny creek zipped around Nautilus' paws and wound through the island. A group of parrots glided overhead, squawking and chirping to one another. *See?* Nautilus told himself. *Everything is fine. No need to panic.*

At least, not until I see the disappointed looks on my friends' faces, he realized with a gulp.

The sound of laughter, chopping, and clanging grew louder and louder as Nautilus wandered deeper into the island. What were his friends up to? "Guys?" Nautilus sheepishly called out. "It's, uh, it's me, Nautilus. I'm back."

The noises abruptly halted. "Nautilus!" came the happy cry of Aurora. She suddenly glided into view and skidded to a halt right in front of him. Her white fur was full of small twigs and leaves, and was streaked with mud. Yeesh. What happened to her?

Aurora smiled brightly. "I'm so excited to see you, Nautilus. How'd it go? How many friends did you make? Tell me everything!" She looked as energetic as a pup. Being able to relax after defeating Queen Tempest was doing wonders for Aurora. Nautilus instantly felt guilty. He was certainly going to ruin her good mood when he confessed his failure. Nautilus opened his mouth to speak, but was thankfully interrupted by Aurora.

"Wait! Before you tell me, come see what Ember and I have been working on." Aurora nudged Nautilus forward. "You're going to love this!" Without waiting for a response, Aurora sprinted away, becoming swallowed up by the jungle foliage. Nautilus hesitated for a long moment, then slowly followed her.

Nautilus found himself in a large clearing. Trees surrounded the cozy meadow on all sides, protecting the area from strong winds. Butterflies lazily floated back and forth, while dragonflies zipped through the air.

Piles of wooden planks were neatly stacked in the corner. They rested closely beside a bonfire, ready to be tossed in whenever the blaze weakened. Roasting above the fire was prey of all kinds. Nautilus' mouth began to water. It smelled delicious.

Dinner wasn't the only thing that impressed Nautilus. Aurora and Ember had started to build a massive treehouse. It was nowhere close to being completed yet, but Nautilus could tell that it was going to look fantastic when it was finished.

"So," Aurora asked giddily. "What do you think?"

Nautilus' eyes were wide. "It's amazing," he whispered. "You two have really... accomplished a lot today." Nautilus felt uncomfortable in his own fur. How could he confess his failure *now*, after seeing everything his friends achieved?

"Thanks, Nautilus," Aurora said sweetly. "Anyway. Tell us about your day. I bet you did awesome!"

At the same moment, Ember appeared. He carried a collection of green fronds in his mouth, and looked just as untidy as Aurora. Nautilus couldn't help but gawk as Ember walked closer. He was wearing a necklace of vibrant flowers. In fact, looking more closely at Aurora, Nautilus realized that she was wearing a matching flower bracelet.

For the moon's sake! They were making each other gifts now. Nautilus had a funny feeling he wouldn't be the only hybrid in Elementa for much longer. He shuddered, imaging winged pups flying through the air while shooting fireballs from their paws.

Ember looked startled to see Nautilus. Embarrassment flooded Ember's face, and he instantly slid his necklace off, hiding it behind a boulder. "Uh, hi, Nautilus," Ember spluttered. "What are you... how did your adventure go?" Ember shifted his paws awkwardly.

What in Elementa is wrong with him?! Nautilus thought, aghast. *He's not grumpy anymore!* "It was fine, I guess," Nautilus responded. He stared down at his paws.

Ember impatiently lashed his tail. "Care to give us any more details?" he snapped. Oh, good. Ember wasn't completely lost yet. Nautilus had been worried.

"Details?" Nautilus choked out. "Are you looking for specific details, or general details? Because there's so much to talk about, I don't even know where to start." Nautilus smiled guiltily.

Ember suspiciously looked Nautilus up and down. "You're stalling," he hissed. "What happened out there?"

Aurora, for the first time in forever, wasn't smiling. Her green-eyed gaze flickered between Ember and Nautilus nervously.

Nautilus took a step back, his heart pounding. "Nothing happened out there," he spluttered. "Nothing completely awful, anyway."

Ember bared his fangs. "Tell us the truth," he snarled. "*Now.*"

Nautilus was tempted to make a run for it, but he knew that he couldn't outpace Ember. Nautilus flattened his ears. His tail drooped. "I... uh... I met only a few Water Wolves," he confessed in a squeaky voice.

"And?" Ember snapped.

Nautilus nervously fiddled with the fins on his tail. "I met their pet shark, too," he continued.

"Obviously you lived," Ember growled impatiently. "Keep going."

"And... I... made a complete fool of myself," Nautilus mumbled.

Ember took a step back, smoothing his bristling, dark red fur. He grinned. "So nothing out of the ordinary, then?" he laughed.

"Hey!" Nautilus cried, offended.

Aurora gave Ember an unhappy look. She then gently placed her wing on Nautilus' shoulder, trying to comfort him. Ember frowned jealously. "What went wrong, Nautilus?" Aurora asked softly. "Are you okay? You didn't get hurt, did you?"

Nautilus shook his head. "It wasn't anything like that," he murmured, feeling a fresh wave of embarrassment and frustration with himself. "I couldn't speak underwater like the rest of the wolves could. They laughed at me. They thought something was wrong with me. And they're right." His voice broke. Tears slid down his face, but he quickly wiped them away. "I don't belong in the ocean. I'm not the right wolf for this task. I'm a failure, and I'm only holding you two back."

Nautilus clenched his jaw. "It would be best if I leave our group for good."

Ember's eyes widened. "Hey, hey, hold on," he said. "Get a grip, Nautilus. Aurora would be heartbroken if you left. I hate to admit this, but I'd miss you, too. You can't leave. I... I won't let you. And seriously. You have got to stop crying. We care about you, okay? Yeesh."

Nautilus' entire face was wet with tears. Snot trickled down his nose. "Really?" he asked. "You mean it? I thought you two would want me gone for sure."

Aurora looked shocked. She flared her wings in alarm and took a protective step closer to Nautilus. "Of course we don't!" she cried. "We would never want you to leave. You're like family to us, Nautilus. We need you."

Nautilus felt like the lowest sea slug in the world. He shrunk underneath Ember's and Aurora's concerned gazes. "But I messed up so badly today," he protested. "You two were counting on me, and I failed you. Aren't you upset?"

"We all make mistakes," Aurora said. She let out a guilty laugh. "I used to think Queen Tempest was my hero. I trusted Fog, the wolf who led all those Sky Pack guards to The Hidden Howl. I accidentally got my brother captured and imprisoned. I gave Queen Tempest enough White Elemental Heart to build her superweapon crown. I've done a number of mistakes. It happens to everyone."

Ember kicked at a loose pebble. "I'm not perfect, either," he mumbled. "I've made terrible mistakes that I'd rather not talk about. I regret what I did every single day." Ember gave his pelt a shake. "The point is, Nautilus, that you keep your chin up and move on."

Nautilus nodded slowly. "You're right," he breathed. "You're both right. I see that now. Thank you for not giving up on me." Nautilus gave Aurora and Ember a shy, toothy smile.

Ember playfully cuffed Nautilus on the ear. "That's the last time you talk about leaving," he said. "You better not even *think* about abandoning us. You're stuck with me and Aurora, whether you like it or not. We're a pack now."

Aurora nodded. "We're not going to let you give up, either," she told Nautilus. "Ember and I believe in you. I know that you're scared and reluctant to go back, but I think you should give the Water Pack a second chance. Don't let your fear win by giving up. Okay?"

Yeesh, Nautilus thought. *I think they'd make better motivational speakers, instead of world-saving heroes.* "Okay," he agreed with a huff. "I'll go back tomorrow morning, if that's what you think is best." Nautilus immediately regretted saying that, but it was too late. His friends were already walking away, heading toward their prey and bonfire.

Nautilus felt queasy and woozy inside, as if he had swallowed a bunch of squirming worms. His paws began to shake as he followed his friends. *At least I can't mess up more than I already have,* Nautilus realized anxiously. *How much worse can things possibly get?*

CHAPTER 4

Nautilus woke up to the bloodcurdling shriek of a parrot. With a gasp, he jumped to his paws. Nautilus accidentally smacked the back of his head on a low hanging tree branch. He groaned, half in pain, and half annoyed. What a terrible start to the already terrible day. Nautilus unhappily rubbed the back of his head with a paw, wincing.

The sky was a pale shade of violet. Long, thin clouds floated above like ribbons. The sun was just beginning to rise above the jungle treetops, giving the many leaves a glowing, golden outline. A warm breeze gently flowed through the meadow, rustling the foliage.

Nautilus yawned. He stood up and stretched, blinking the sleepiness from his light green eyes.

On the far side of the clearing, Aurora and Ember slept side-by-side, underneath their uncompleted treehouse. Aurora's wing was wrapped over Ember like a blanket of feathers. Ember's black cloak was tucked into a compact ball underneath Aurora's head, appearing to be a pillow. The two wolves looked happy, even while asleep.

I won't let you guys down, Nautilus silently told them. *Not again. I'll be a wolf worth keeping around. I promise.* He turned around and walked away, careful to make as little noise as possible. His long tail flattened the tall grass as it dragged behind him. Nautilus pushed past the meadow's edge and entered the jungle.

Dragonflies zipped past Nautilus as he made his way to the beach. *Oh, I hope I don't make a fool of myself again today,* he thought. *Maybe it would be best if I just keep to myself, and stay out of the Water Wolves' way. Yes. That sounds like a good plan. I'll avoid everyone as much as possible, and focus on understanding and observing their way of life. I could discover some helpful information that way.*

When Nautilus reached the jungle's edge, he halted, staring out at the ocean with wide eyes. *I can do this,* Nautilus told himself. *I'll be okay. If I can survive a battle with Queen Tempest, I can survive the Water Pack. I just need to imagine myself as Sandstorm again today. She's tough, brave, and not scared of anything. I'll be just like her!*

Nautilus strode toward the ocean, a salty breeze buffeting his dark blue fur. Despite adopting Sandstorm's confidence, his heart still began to pound. Nautilus' pawsteps faltered. Memories began to swirl through his head, reminding him of all his embarrassments the day before. The laughing Water Wolves. How the shark had trapped him between its teeth. The moment everyone had stared at him suspiciously, knowing with certainty that something was wrong with him.

Nautilus froze, just out of the waves' reach. *I can't do this!* he thought fearfully. *I'm too afraid. Afraid of the Water Wolves, and afraid of failing. What will the Water Pack Empire do to me if they discover the truth? I'm a hybrid, a wolf who doesn't belong in the divided world of Elementa. How can I risk exposing myself? Those wolves from yesterday could tell instantly that I was different. How many mistakes will it take for them to figure out what I really am?* Nautilus felt sick.

Suddenly, the foliage behind Nautilus began to rustle. Ember appeared. He walked toward the beach, looking peaceful and eager to start the day. "Oh, hey Nautilus," Ember said when he spotted him. "Good morning."

Nautilus waved half-heartedly. "Good morning," he replied. "Um, what are you doing?"

Ember had sauntered right past Nautilus and entered the ocean. Ember only came to a stop once the water was up to his knees. "Fishing," he responded distractedly. "You?"

Nautilus fiddled with the fins on his tail. "I'm going back to the Water Pack Empire, I guess," he mumbled. Wanting to avoid looking like a coward, Nautilus slowly entered the ocean. He briefly paused beside

Ember. "See you and Aurora later." With a sigh, Nautilus continued forward.

Ember was silent for a moment. "Hey, wait," he said, just before Nautilus plunged his head underwater. "I want to tell you something before you go."

Nautilus forced back a groan. *This ought to be good,* he thought sarcastically. Nautilus turned around and paddled back toward Ember. "Is everything okay?" he asked.

Ember kept his eyes on the ocean, not wanting to miss an approaching fish. "No," Ember bluntly responded. "Everything is not okay, and it's pretty much all your fault."

Nautilus winced. "Oh," he whispered.

"You want to know why?" Ember continued sharply. "Because you're *letting* yourself be afraid. I wasn't completely honest with you yesterday, because I knew Aurora would be unhappy with me. But now that it's just you and me, I'm going to speak my mind."

Nautilus sunk lower in the water. He was not liking where this was going.

Ember's jaw clenched. "Nautilus, you have it so easy," he spat. "You think life is so hard for you, but it's not. You're a hybrid, for the moon's sake! You have two packs. Two identities. Two chances to make life good for yourself."

Nautilus blinked. He kept quiet, waiting for Ember to continue.

"I know I've been hiding my past from you and Aurora," Ember growled, "but let me tell you one thing. Growing up wasn't fun for me. I wish I could be a hybrid like you. My life in the Fire Pack was broken and beyond repair. If I had another face, and the chance to become another wolf, I could have started over." Ember's flanks rose and fell with every sharp, angry breath he took. "Listen to me carefully, Nautilus. If you mess up in the Water Pack, it's no big deal. That's the truth. I'm not saying that to be nice. I'm saying that to be honest."

Ember abruptly met Nautilus' gaze. He took a dangerous step forward. "Transform into a Fire Wolf," Ember ordered.

Nautilus changed instantly, not wanting to get on Ember's bad side. The water immediately began to heat up around Nautilus' scorching paws. Ember glared at Nautilus. "Quit gawking at me and look at your reflection," he snarled.

Nautilus looked down at the ocean's clear surface. He was silent for a long time as he stared at his reflection. Nautilus barely recognized his Fire Wolf appearance. He always preferred being a Water Wolf, since his webbed paws couldn't accidentally light anything on fire. It was strange seeing himself like this.

Nautilus' Fire Wolf form had a leaner face, with sharper, yellow eyes. His ears were more pointed, and his snout looked less crooked.

"Who are you?" Ember abruptly demanded.

"Um, I'm Nautilus," he sheepishly responded.

"No, you're not," Ember hissed. "You're not Nautilus anymore. You don't have to be him. You can be someone different now. An entirely new life is yours for the taking, whenever you want it."

Nautilus' eyes grew wide. His heartbeat quickened.

Ember lashed his tail. "Stop worrying about messing things up in the Water Pack," he continued firmly. "If things go wrong there, you don't have to be an outcast like me. You have another pack waiting for you, where nobody is aware of your mistakes. You have the rare opportunity to start life over. Be grateful for that gift. Embrace it every moment of every day. It's more precious than gold."

The water around Nautilus' paws began to boil. Tiny, white bubbles drifted through the ocean waves. If Ember was in pain from the heat, he didn't show it. "That's... really good advice," Nautilus confessed. "I've always been ashamed of being a hybrid. It's never been something that I've viewed as a gift. Not until now." Nautilus felt weak with relief. "I was so scared about ruining my life. I never realized that I have a clean slate waiting for me, if something does go wrong in the Water Pack."

Ember was silent for a long moment. Bitterness and jealously were written all over his face, and he didn't even try hiding it. Ember wanted everything Nautilus had. Ember probably thought that Nautilus didn't deserve his gifts. However, Ember's response was kind. "Will you stop worrying about everything going wrong now?" he asked.

Nautilus nodded. "I'll do my best," he replied. "I'm not as afraid of the Water Pack anymore. It's like a weight has been lifted off of my shoulders. Ember, I can't thank you enough."

Ember looked away. "It's fine," he grumbled.

Nautilus gave his Fire Wolf reflection one last look. *I can be someone different, if I want to be,* he thought happily. *I can have a brand new life in the Fire Pack. I don't have to fear everything going wrong anymore. I have two chances to make my life awesome.* He studied his reflection carefully. *I think my Fire Wolf name will be... Singe. It suites me.*

"Ember?" came the distant call of Aurora. "Ember, where are you?"

"I'm over here!" Ember responded cheerfully, his mood lifting instantly. Nautilus could tell that Ember truly loved Aurora. They made each other happy.

"What?" Ember said, noticing the look on Nautilus' face. "Why are you smiling like a big goof?"

"No reason," Nautilus said innocently. He transformed back into a Water Wolf. *I'm just happy to see you happy,* he thought. *You deserve it, after everything that went on in your life. Maybe wolves can have a happy ending, after all.*

Aurora suddenly glided into view. She spotted Nautilus and Ember, then swooped down to land on the beach in front of them. "Hey, Nautilus," Aurora called. "You look... excited."

Nautilus nodded enthusiastically. "I am," he responded happily. "Ember and I were just talking. I had no idea he could give such good life advice. He's a really awesome wolf. You're lucky to have him, Aurora."

Ember blushed, looking furious and embarrassed all at once. "Nautilus," he groaned. "Knock it off."

Aurora giggled. "So," she said, changing the subject. "Are you off to the Water Pack now?"

Nautilus nodded happily. "Yup," he said. "And I'm not afraid to go anymore."

Aurora's eyes widened. "Really?" she cooed. "I'm impressed. Ember must have really given some good advice." Aurora winked teasingly at him, managing to make Ember look even more flustered than before.

Nautilus laughed. "See you two later," he said. Nautilus turned around, then swam away from the shores of Emora Island. Once he could no longer touch the bottom with his paws, Nautilus plunged his head underwater, entering the sea.

Tropical fish of all shapes and sizes glided past Nautilus. Vibrant coral reefs decorated the ocean floor. A warm current swooshed around Nautilus, propelling him forward. He swam with confidence, no longer needing to impersonate Sandstorm. Nautilus, thanks to Ember's help, had found his own courage. It was one of the best feelings in the world.

Before long, Nautilus reached the kelp forest that marked the beginning of the Water Pack Empire. Although it was natural for Nautilus to feel worried, he found that his emotions no longer controlled him. Nautilus breezily entered the kelp forest, swimming through it with newfound confidence.

He soon emerged on the other side, finding himself face-to-face with the magnificent Water Pack Empire. It took Nautilus' very breath away. The dazzling empire stretched vastly across the ocean floor. Although Nautilus was far away from the kingdom, he could see the vast amount of wealth put into its construction. Jewels, gems, and riches of all kinds decorated the buildings. It made the empire look like a massive heap of treasure.

Hundreds upon thousands of Water Wolves swam from place to place, making the underwater kingdom look bustling and alive. Nautilus gulped. He felt intimated by the sight of all those unknown wolves. They were all strangers to him.

I don't need to be afraid of the Water Wolves anymore, Nautilus reminded himself. *This isn't the only place I can belong. If all else fails, I can turn to the Fire Pack. I have two chances to make my life great.* He released a deep breath. *And if I blow it at both packs, I can always go back to my den at the lagoon, and forget this whole adventure even happened.*

Nautilus bravely swam forward. He didn't look back once. *I have a feeling that everything is going to work out fine,* he thought.

CHAPTER 5

Oh, wow, Nautilus thought in awe. *This place is spectacular!*

Nautilus had reached the outskirts of the Water Pack Empire, hesitating before he officially swam inside the border. Massive, spiraling towers stuck out of the ocean floor like dazzling, jewel encrusted claws. Nautilus could hear cheerful music playing inside the kingdom, while countless voices of chattering Water Wolves filled the ocean.

With wide eyes, Nautilus swam a few paces forward. *Will anyone stop me from entering the empire?* he wondered cautiously. Nautilus looked around, scanning his surroundings. *There's no gates or barricades. I can't see a single guard anywhere. No weapons, either.* This was completely different from the other packs in Elementa. *I guess the Water Wolves don't need to worry about invaders, since they're safe underneath the ocean waves.*

Nautilus warily looked around again. It felt strange to have the ability to swim right into a foreign kingdom, without even being questioned by its inhabitants. *This is my home, too,* Nautilus reminded himself. *I'm an inhabitant of the Water Pack Empire if*

I choose to be. I probably have family that lives here, for Elementa's sake.

Nautilus inhaled a deep breath, his gills fluttering. Then, exhaling, he swam toward the Water Pack, ready to enter it for the very first time. *Here goes nothing,* Nautilus thought, feeling exhilarated and nervous all at once. *Just remember what Ember told me. It won't be the end of the world if I can't find my place in the Water Pack. The only thing that matters is that I do my best.*

The tall towers caused shadows to fall over Nautilus as he approached them. His heartbeat began to quicken. Nautilus expected guards to suddenly appear and attack him at any moment. However, all was peaceful. Surprisingly peaceful. Nautilus was pleasantly surprised. *Maybe things will work out after all,* he thought.

Nautilus came face-to-face with a row of long, complex alleyways. *Huh,* he thought, pausing to study the entrances closest to him. *Which one to choose... This alleyway has seashells decorating the ground. I like seashells. All right, this one it is.* Nautilus entered the passageway immediately, before he could scare himself out of it. He swam through the alley, his paws and tail swishing the water around him. *This is so exciting, and totally not terrifying at all. I just need to remember Ember's advice. I'm fine. Everything is fine. I've got this.*

Nautilus kept on swimming, forcing himself to not look back. Whenever an anxious thought popped into his head, Nautilus briskly pushed it back down, trying to avoid thinking about anything that wasn't positive. *I'm home,* Nautilus told himself, a bit forcefully to squash down his nerves. A weak smile appeared on his face. *One of my homes, at least.*

After what felt like an eternity of navigating through the complex labyrinth of alleyways, Nautilus spotted light at the end of the tunnel. Literally. Nautilus had finally reached the end. *Oh, great!* he thought in exasperation. *I thought I was lost.*

The upbeat music and cheerful voices were as loud as ever now. The entirety of the Water Pack Empire was just on the other side of this passage. Nautilus was finally about to face his pack at long last. *Okay. This is it. Stop freaking out, Nautilus. Deep breaths. No, don't stop swimming. You've got to go. Keep going. Almost there. Breathe. Stay calm.*

Nautilus released a long, shuddering breath.

Sunlight fell over his fur as he emerged on the other side. He froze, his mouth falling open. *Oh. My. Goodness,* Nautilus thought. *It's... it's amazing!*

Nautilus was right in the heart of the empire. Aquatic plants of all shapes and sizes decorated the greenspace, while towers of gold and silver surrounded the area on all sides. The buildings sparkled dazzlingly in the warm rays of the sun.

Nautilus slowly swam forward, feeling astonished. *I think this is a park,* he realized. Vibrant patches of coral dappled the sea floor. Long strands of kelp were tied together at the base, while the tops freely flowed in the gentle current, giving the appearance of flowy trees. Pathways of seashells and pearls looped and spiraled in every direction. Nautilus even spotted a few miniature rock gardens here and there.

Water Wolves were everywhere Nautilus looked. Some rested underneath the shade of the kelp trees, looking carefree and peaceful. Others tossed what appeared to be disks back and forth to each other. A few wolves were even playing a type of instrument that Nautilus had never seen before.

A group of three pups abruptly swooshed past Nautilus. He instinctively shuffled backward, shrinking in his own fur. "Tag!" one of the pups cried, as she patted her friend with a paw. "You're it!" The three pups giggled as they zoomed away. Nautilus watched them without moving. *They hadn't even looked at me,* he thought. *In fact, nobody is looking at me. They aren't acting like I'm anything out of the ordinary. It's like I'm welcome here. Like I belong. This is great!*

Nautilus couldn't help but smile. The cheerful energy of the Water Pack coursed through his veins, filling him with joy and confidence. With barely a hint of worry, Nautilus glided forward, entering the community of Water Wolves. He swam along one of the paths, allowing it to lead him anywhere. Nautilus wasn't concerned about where he was going. He wanted to see everything the Water Pack Empire had to offer. This was one of the rare times when getting lost was actually fun.

Up ahead, two Water Wolfs suddenly veered onto Nautilus' pathway, swimming toward him. Nautilus' heart began to race. *Ack!* he thought. *What do I do?! Should I hide? Should I ignore them? Do Water Wolves have a special greeting that I don't know about?* Before Nautilus could panic any further, the wolves did something extraordinary—something that Nautilus would never forget.

They smiled and said, "Hello."

Then, the Water Wolves swam right by, leaving him with nothing but a friendly greeting. No glares. No rude comments. No suspicious looks. Nautilus was in shock.

Sure, it wasn't exactly 'extraordinary', but the simple gesture had meant everything to Nautilus. *They thought I was normal,* he thought happily. *No stranger had ever said 'hello' to me before. That was amazing!*

Nautilus found himself waving a bit too enthusiastically at every wolf that crossed his path. The wolves happily waved back each time. Nautilus thought that his heart would explode from all the joy it was experiencing. If this was a dream, Nautilus hoped that he never woke up. *I think this is the best day of my life,* he thought giddily.

After a few minutes of waving and swimming, Nautilus spotted a group of pups huddled around an older wolf. "Repeat after me," he said. "Ocean."

The pups blurted out a plethora of responses, most of which didn't sound anything close to 'ocean'. Nautilus slowed, staring at the pups. Most of their voices had sounded strange and choked... just like Nautilus' voice, whenever he attempted to speak underwater.

The teacher grinned. "Most of you seem to be having trouble with that one," he said kindly. "No worries. You'll all get there soon. Remember, when speaking underwater, you need to rely on your gills."

Nautilus swam closer, halting a respectful distance away from the class. *I can't believe my luck,* Nautilus thought. *A lesson just for speaking underwater. This is perfect!* Nautilus was beyond embarrassed to be in the same level as a bunch of newborn pups, but listened attentively nonetheless. Thankfully, nobody seemed to notice Nautilus. At least, that's what Nautilus thought.

"Let's try another word," said the teacher. "Remember to pay attention to how I use both my gills *and* my mouth to speak. Repeat after me: Kelp."

Nautilus watched the teacher's movements carefully, then whispered, "Kelp." Nautilus smiled so much that his face began to hurt. *I did it!* he thought triumphantly. *I said my first word underwater! Sure, it sounded a bit off, but I still did it!*

Before long, Nautilus' underwater linguistic skills were close to perfect. It still felt awkward and unnatural to speak with his gills, but he managed it nevertheless. "Fish," he whispered. "Sea. Wave. Coral." Nautilus paused, trying to think of more practical words and phrases that could help him during his time underwater. "Hello. Goodbye. Yes. No. Nautilus. Please. Thanks. Good. Happy." Nautilus felt warm from ears to tail. "I'm so happy."

Nautilus was proud of himself. It was something that rarely happened, but Nautilus felt like now was a deserving moment. He'd actually managed to accomplish something without messing up. It was one of the best feelings in the world. Now, he could communicate with his fellow Water Wolves, and not have to worry about embarrassing himself.

Feeling confident in his newfound abilities, Nautilus left the class behind, continuing along the pathway. "Hello," Nautilus cheerfully told a passing wolf. "Good afternoon."

"Good afternoon," the wolf responded warmly.

Nautilus nearly squealed with delight. *I can't believe I was so worried about nothing,* he thought. *Now that I'm in the Water Pack, I'm thinking I might have a place here after all. The empire could be my new home.*

Nautilus eventually left the park behind, feeling brave enough to venture into the city. He felt awestruck by the sheer amount of wolves. There were so many of them, all packed together in one community. Nautilus had never seen so many individuals in one place before. It was easy to be overwhelmed by it all, even with Nautilus' new self-assurance.

I can do this, Nautilus told himself. *Besides, what's the worst that can possibly happen? As long as I blend in, everything will be fine.*

The underwater city was unlike anything Nautilus had ever seen before. The towers each had dozens of balconies, storefronts to their own individual shops. Nautilus couldn't see a single flight of stairs anywhere. *I guess if a wolf wants to get to the higher floors, all they have to do is swim up,* he realized.

Beside each balcony door was a large, bright and vibrant sign. They were clearly designed to catch the eye of a customer. One sign in particular snagged Nautilus' attention immediately. It featured artwork of a big orange fish. Nautilus' mouth started to water. *A restaurant,* he thought. *Perfect. I'm starving.* He swam toward the shop, hoping they served sushi.

"Greetings," said the shopkeeper, once Nautilus paddled inside. "How can I help you today? Are you looking for anything in particular?" The shopkeeper had tentacles instead of arms, and wore a pair of crooked glasses.

Other than the shopkeeper and Nautilus, there were only a few other Water Wolves inside the store. Most were pups, and the rest appeared to be their parents. Fish lazily swam around in circles, looking pampered and sluggish. Nautilus eyed them hungrily. Before Nautilus could respond to the shopkeeper, one of the pups let out a delighted squeal. "Can I get this one? Pretty please?" he asked his parents. "I promise I'll take good care of it."

Strange, Nautilus thought. *I've never heard someone talk about taking 'good care' of their dinner before. It must be a Water Wolf thing.*

"I'm okay, thank you," Nautilus politely told the shopkeeper. "Don't go out of your way for me. I'll catch my own fish."

The shopkeeper nervously adjusted her glasses. "Catch?" she echoed. "What do you mean by..."

Nautilus suddenly caught one of the fish between his paws. It squirmed angrily in Nautilus' grasp. "This one looks tasty!" he exclaimed. "Do you do takeout?" Nautilus' cheeks began to burn. Everyone was gawking at him like he had just sprouted another head. "What?" Nautilus asked sheepishly. He shrunk in his dark blue fur.

A thought suddenly struck Nautilus. He managed to become even more embarrassed than before. "Oh, I just remembered something," Nautilus spluttered. "I, uh, don't have any money to pay you. Sorry about that." Nautilus released the fish, then hurriedly swam outside. How humiliating!

Nautilus returned to the stream of bustling Water Wolves, allowing himself to become one with their flow of movement. *Stop worrying, Nautilus,* he scolded himself as he swam. *It wasn't that bad. I'm sure plenty of wolves forget their money all the time. Right? Right.* Nautilus nervously rubbed the back of his neck with a paw. *I wonder if I'll need to get a job, since I might be living here one day.* The thought made Nautilus shudder. He'd rather bask in the sun than spend his days working his paws to the bone.

A beam of blinding light suddenly hit Nautilus right in the eyes. "Ouch!" he gasped, trying to shield his face from the intense glow. *What in Elementa?! That's so painful! What is causing all that light?* Nautilus squinted so much that his eyes were nearly closed. However, he managed to see the source of light, and it made his heart race.

There was a colossal castle up ahead, decorated with jewels from top to bottom.

The castle was, without a doubt, the grandest and largest building in the entire Water Pack Empire. It was so tall that it nearly stuck out of the ocean altogether. Sunlight shone directly onto the gold and silver fortress, making it glitter with a million tiny stars. On both sides of the castle rested two enormous statues depicting Water Wolves. One of the wolves held a gigantic trident, and had a fierce expression on her face. The other wolf had a calmer expression, and he carried a scroll in one paw, and a pen in the other.

Nautilus was transfixed by the castle. It took a few moments for his eyes to adjust to the brightness, but when they did, he felt amazed all over again. Nautilus had never seen anything so outstanding in all his life. For a moment, he allowed himself to wonder what it would be like to live in such a marvelous castle. *Wouldn't it be hilarious if my Water Wolf parent happened to be royalty?* he thought. Nautilus nearly laughed at the idea. *As if.*

Nautilus broke away from the endless stream of travelling Water Wolves, deciding to get a better look at the castle. He swam toward the entrance, wondering if he was allowed to go inside. Two guards were posted by the grand doorway, looking stern and menacing. However, they were silent as wolves quietly swam in and out of the castle.

The visitors all looked common, and no different from Nautilus. Perhaps every Water Pack citizen was allowed to view the castle's interior. Nautilus decided he'd better ask, just to be safe.

"Um, excuse me," Nautilus said to the guards. "Am I allowed to go inside?"

To Nautilus' surprise, the guards' faces shifted from serious to bewildered in a matter of seconds. However, they didn't say a word. All they did was stare. Nautilus flattened his ears, feeling just as flustered as the guards looked.

There was awkward silence for a long, long moment. Nautilus, feeling completely weirded out, swam into the castle. They hadn't told Nautilus that he *wasn't* allowed to go inside.

There were at least a hundred wolves scattered throughout the castle's lobby. They swam cautiously, not uttering a single word. Nautilus scarcely noticed them, instead focusing on the majesty of the castle and the artwork that decorated it.

"This place is awesome!" Nautilus exclaimed. His voice sliced through the silence—causing everyone to immediately stare at him in horror.

Nautilus wanted to gasp and hide and cry at the same time. His pelt burned with embarrassment. "Uh, sorry," Nautilus whispered. He decided to turn around and swim away, unsure of what else to do in such a bizarre situation. Nautilus burst out of the castle and entered the noisy, lively city, feeling relieved to escape the strange silence.

What was wrong with all those wolves? Nautilus wondered, aghast. *Why wasn't anyone speaking? I would've thought that such a dazzling castle would be home to parties and feasts. It was like a ghost town in there!*

Nautilus' heart was still pounding from the humiliating experience. He suddenly felt tired, hungry, and ready for a long nap. *I think that's enough exploring for one day,* Nautilus thought. *All things considering, I don't think I did too badly today. I can speak underwater now, and I'm more familiar with the empire. I'll call that a success.*

Nautilus headed back to the aquatic park, ready to leave the Water Pack Empire and return to Emora Island. He was completely unaware of the guards that were stalking him from the shadows. Nautilus was being watched.

CHAPTER 6

Nautilus woke up in a surprisingly good mood. No nightmares had tormented him like they normally did, which lifted Nautilus' spirits drastically. Instead of having worrisome dreams of running away from unseen enemies, Nautilus had dreamt of making new friends in the Water Pack, and of exploring the vast ocean.

Nautilus rose to his paws then gave his pelt a shake. A crisp breeze flowed through the meadow, rustling the nearby jungle trees. A flock of vibrant macaws glided overhead. Nautilus inhaled a deep breath, smiling. Today, Nautilus could tell, was going to be a great day.

On the far side of the clearing, Aurora was continuing construction on the treehouse. It was coming along nicely, and was almost complete. Not too far away was Ember, who was rubbing two twigs together in an attempt to create a campfire. Nautilus felt a twinge of pity for his friend. If only Ember had an elemental power. He could've created hundreds of fires by now.

Nautilus was tempted to transform into a Fire Wolf, so he could light the fire for Ember. However, he didn't dare, knowing that Ember would only take the gesture the wrong way.

After a few minutes of struggling, Ember eventually managed to create a small spark. It travelled throughout the pile of firewood, creating a cozy blaze. Nautilus smiled at the thrilled look on Ember's face.

Nautilus sauntered closer to his friends. "Good morning," he greeted warmly.

Aurora leapt off her wooden platform and glided down to meet Nautilus. "Morning!" she replied, landing in front of him. "Are you off to the Water Pack Empire now?"

Nautilus grinned. "Yeah," he replied. "I wish you two could come with me. It's really awesome there."

Ember strode to Aurora's side, who wrapped a wing around him. "We'll take your word for it," Ember haughtily told Nautilus. "I'm just glad you aren't freaking out about going to the empire anymore. It's a *huge* relief. I'd thought you'd never toughen up." Ember gave him a condescending look.

Nautilus' jaw clenched, ever so slightly. Why was Ember acting smug all of a sudden? It wasn't like him to talk down to Nautilus. What had come over his friend?

Trying to avoid starting a fight, Nautilus forced on a smile. "Your advice really helped me," he replied. "Thanks, Ember."

Ember gave him a stiff nod. "It was nothing," he muttered.

There was an uncomfortable pause for a moment. Nautilus, feeling completely weirded out, took a step back. "I'll see you guys tonight," he mumbled sheepishly. "Bye."

Aurora waved cheerily, while Ember simply watched Nautilus go without a trace of emotion on his face. Nautilus felt itchy, like bugs were crawling through his fur. He could only wonder what thoughts were running through Ember's head. It was no secret that Ember believed he deserved everything Nautilus had. Was he angry with him?

It's not my fault that I'm a hybrid, Nautilus thought in frustration. He headed toward the beach with a scowl on his face. *And it isn't my fault that Ember doesn't have a power. He can be upset all he wants. It's not like it'll change anything.*

Tropical leaves slid across Nautilus' fur as he stepped out of the jungle. Soft, white sand squelched beneath his paws as he made his way to the ocean. Sunlight shone onto the waves, causing them to sparkle. Nautilus felt much more excited than he thought he would to return to the Water Pack Empire.

He almost felt as if he was... going home. Nautilus' heart fluttered at the thought, distracting him from his worries about Ember's snarky new attitude.

He stepped into the ocean, relishing the salty breeze as it danced around his pelt, Nautilus kept on walking until the water reached his shoulders. Just before he could plunge his head beneath the waves, a voice cried out, "Wait!"

Aurora flew out of the jungle and swooped toward Nautilus. He braced himself for impact, expecting her to crash down right on top of him. However, Aurora pulled herself into a hover just above his head. The powerful flaps of her wings caused an explosion of ripples. Droplets flew in every direction. Nautilus' eyes were wide. "Is everything okay?" he spluttered, struggling to make himself heard over the thunderous beats of her wings.

"*What?*" Aurora shouted, unable to hear him. She abruptly tucked in her wings. Aurora cannoned into the water beside him, creating a torrent of white bubbles. Nautilus was pushed backward by the impact. He floundered for a moment, struggling to regain his balance. Then, once the water calmed, Nautilus paddled to Aurora.

"Is everything okay?" Nautilus repeated. "What's the matter?"

Aurora gave him a toothy grin. Her wings were spread out at her sides, keeping her afloat. "Nothing's the matter," Aurora replied nonchalantly. "It's just that I almost forgot to give you something." She lifted one of her paws out of the water. Concern spilled across her face. "Shoot," she hissed. "I think I dropped it in the water."

Nautilus immediately dove under the waves, scanning the ocean floor. He quickly spotted something wooden. Nautilus scooped it up with one webbed paw, then resurfaced. "Is this it?" he asked, holding it out to show Aurora.

Aurora smiled. "It is," she said. "Happy birthday, Nautilus!"

Nautilus felt flustered and confused all at once. "Birthday?" he echoed numbly. "Is it my birthday today? If it is, I completely forgot about it..."

"Well, it probably isn't," Aurora confessed awkwardly. "You've never told Ember and I when your birthday is, so we just kind of guessed." Aurora watched a tiny fish as it swam around her paws. "I was chatting with Ember last night, and we realized that it's been one whole year since the three of us met at The Hidden Howl. We've never celebrated your birthday once, Nautilus, so we decided to make you a little gift. I hope you like it."

Nautilus looked away from Aurora and turned his attention to the object in his paws. The bracelet was connected to a smooth piece of bark that had a painting of three messy, scribbled wolves. One of the wolves was painted in white, and was clearly supposed to be Aurora. The second wolf, who had a gooty expression and stood in the middle, was blue. It wasn't hard for Nautilus to tell that it was supposed to be him. The third wolf was red, and was obviously Ember.

"I painted it," Aurora said proudly. "But Ember made the rest of it." She pointed a claw at the painting of Ember. "Do you like the grumpy expression I gave him?" Aurora laughed.

Nautilus was pretty sure that his heart had melted. "I love it," he whispered. "I love everything about it." Nautilus slid the bracelet over his wrist, feeling like the happiest wolf in the entire world. "Nobody has ever given me a gift before. In fact, I've never even celebrated my birthday before. I was so young when my parents left me, I was never told when my birthday is. But I think I'll celebrate it today, every year."

Nautilus began to cry. Not wanting Aurora to see his tears, he pulled her into a hug, hiding his face. "Thank you so much, Aurora," he sniffled.

Aurora patted him on the back. "Of course," she replied happily. "It's what friends do." Aurora suddenly pulled back. "Oh! I almost forgot. The bracelet is waterproof, so you can take it with you on your underwater adventures. That way, it's like the three of us aren't apart."

Yup. Nautilus' heart definitely melted. "I'll never take it off," he vowed. "I'll treasure it forever." Nautilus felt a stab of guilt. Perhaps he'd been overreacting about Ember. "Aurora? Please tell Ember that I really appreciate this gift. Tell him that it means a lot to me."

"I will," Aurora promised. "You should've seen Ember while he was making the bracelet. He wouldn't settle for anything but the best. Ember really wanted to make you happy."

Nautilus blinked, feeling surprised. "Really?" he asked.

"Yeah," Aurora said. "Ember tries to hide it, but he's really sweet and kind. I know he acts grumpy sometimes, but I think that's just a shield he puts on to protect himself. Now that Ember and I have grown closer, he's been telling me a bit about his past."

Aurora's ears flattened. "I know he wouldn't want me telling you this, but I think you deserve to know, Nautilus. Ember was hurt badly growing up. Ember's mother never paid attention to him and his siblings, and she disappeared one day without telling anyone. Ember told me his father was ruthless and cruel, especially once they figured out that Ember didn't have an elemental power. Ember had to run away from the Fire Pack to save his life."

Aurora frowned. "I noticed that Ember was talking down to you earlier," she continued. "You did the right thing by repaying rudeness with kindness. Thank you for cutting Ember some slack. He's struggling to have friends after so many hardships. It'll take time for him to fully heal." Aurora gave Nautilus a weak smile. "I know he didn't deserve your patience, but you gave him some anyway. That was a big thing to do."

Nautilus looked away, feeling embarrassed. "I'd better get going now," he murmured. "Thank you again for the bracelet. It really means the world to me."

Aurora smiled. "Of course," she replied. "See you later. Be back before nightfall if you can. I'm going to make Jungle Soup Surprise for dinner!"

Nautilus smirked. "What's the surprise?" he asked.

Aurora stuck her tongue out at him. "It wouldn't be much of a surprise if I told you," she joked. "Now what are you waiting for? Get going and explore the empire!" Aurora teasingly splashed Nautilus.

He smiled as he plunged his head underwater and dove, swimming toward the Water Pack. His bracelet bobbed up and down in the current. *Today is going to be the best unofficial birthday ever,* Nautilus thought. *I can tell that good things are going to come my way.*

***

Apparently, good things weren't going to come Nautilus' way.

Everyone was staring at him. Avoiding him. Whispering about him.

Nautilus swam through the streets of the Water Pack Empire, feeling uncomfortable in his own fur. It was a completely different experience from the day before. Not a single Water Wolf spoke to him. Whenever Nautilus caught someone watching him, they would look away immediately, as if they were afraid to meet Nautilus' gaze.

Why are they so scared of me? he wondered anxiously. *I know I messed up a little bit yesterday, but was it really so bad that the entire empire now knows about my mistakes?* Nautilus wanted to turn invisible and hide forever.

As Nautilus swam along in unspeakable shame, he overheard gossip about him. It was like a slash of claws every time, wounding Nautilus' courage and confidence. All of his old anxiety plummeted down on him like a boulder, crushing him with its weight.

"It's the Pet Chewer," someone whispered.

"Here comes the Silence Breaker," another murmured.

"That weirdo needed lessons from a kindergarten class," someone sneered.

"He doesn't belong here."

"He isn't one of us."

"Stranger." "Outcast." "Freak."

Nautilus began to hyperventilate. Black stars swarmed his vision. His gills fluttered frantically as he struggled to breathe. Nautilus' chest felt tight. He became dizzy. Too many eyes were on him. So many wolves were whispering about him. So much. It was all so much.

Nautilus swam faster than before. He needed to get out of here. He needed to hide. Escape. Flee. *Hurry,* Nautilus urged himself. *Hurry!*

Nautilus had failed. This was a living nightmare. Nautilus had ruined his chance of making a life for himself in the Water Pack. This could no longer be his home. He had made too many mistakes. Wolves had noticed him for all the wrong reasons.

Nautilus' heart pounded violently. *Hurry!* he screamed at himself. Nautilus began to zoom through the empire, swimming blindly. He didn't care where he ended up, as long as it was a world away from here. Nautilus could no longer stay in the Water Pack Empire. He needed to leave *now*.

Tears welled up in his eyes, turning the world blurry. Then—

"GET OUT OF THE WAY!"

Nautilus blinked his eyes back into focus. He gasped. Nautilus had swum right in front of a speeding chariot! The two dolphins that were pulling it veered out of the way at the last moment. Before Nautilus could even react, the chariot slammed right into him.

Nautilus was immediately knocked out. He wasn't sure how much time had passed before he woke up again, but when he did, he found himself in a haze of blood. Nautilus nearly fainted again. Luckily, the source of blood was only from a nosebleed. Pain seared Nautilus' snout. He groaned.

A massive crowd of wolves had gathered around the scene, all unsure of what to do. Whispers. There were so many whispers. Nautilus found himself hoping he would faint again, just to escape the embarrassment.

A few tail lengths away from Nautilus was the chariot, turned upside down. The dolphins were nowhere to be seen, having gotten loose during the collision. However, the Water Wolf that had been inside the chariot was still here.

He looked similar to Nautilus, but instead of having a fish tail, he had a tail resembling that of a shark's. His steel-blue fur was bristling furiously. Rage was spilling over his yellow eyes. Nautilus could tell instantly that this wolf hated him.

The Water Wolf swam to Nautilus, then heaved him off the sea floor, only stopping once they were eye-level. "What in Elementa is wrong with you?" he hissed. "Who are you?"

Nautilus was too weak to break away from the Water Wolf's grasp. "Nautilus," he choked out. "I'm really sorry. Are you okay?"

He managed to look more furious than before. "Do you not know who I am?" he snarled, roughly shaking Nautilus like a ragdoll. "Are you not aware of what you have just done?"

I've probably caused the biggest nosebleed in history, Nautilus thought sarcastically. *But other than that, you seem to be all right.* "I'm sorry," Nautilus croaked. He opened his mouth to continue, but found himself too weak to muster another word.

The Water Wolf pulled back his lips to reveal his jagged fangs, snarling. "I'm Prince Benthos of the Water Pack Empire," he spat, "and you have just embarrassed me in front of all my subjects. I'll have your head for this!"

Fear filled Nautilus' veins, making him cold. His terror gave him enough strength to escape. In a flash, Nautilus broke free from Prince Benthos, then swam away as fast as his weak body allowed. Luckily, nobody seemed to follow Nautilus as he fled the empire. Before long, he found himself in the open ocean.

Nautilus didn't bother looking back at the Water Pack Empire. There was nothing there for him now. He kept on swimming, knowing that he would never return to his former pack. *I've really done it this time,* Nautilus thought grimly. He lightly ran a claw over his bracelet. *This is the worst unofficial birthday ever.*

CHAPTER 7

Nautilus' pelt was dripping with salt water. His pawsteps were clumsy and weak as he dragged himself to the centre of Emora Island. Nautilus was on the verge of collapse.

Wasn't this supposed to be a fun, lighthearted adventure? he asked himself, his teeth clenched. *I should've been making friends and having the time of my life. Instead, I embarrassed myself in front of the entire empire, and got on the wrong side of a prince. To top that off, I got hit by a chariot, for Elementa's sake! How could things have gone so wrong?*

Nautilus' vision was swaying in and out of focus. Through the ringing of his ears, he could hear the cheerful chattering of Aurora and Ember in the distance. Good. He had almost reached the camp.

After what felt like an eternity and a half, Nautilus finally stumbled through the last of the jungle's trees, emerging into the meadow.

Aurora and Ember were sitting side-by-side on the treehouse's balcony, watching the sunset. Aurora was the first to notice Nautilus' arrival. "Nautilus," she cheerily greeted. He collapsed immediately. "Nautilus!" Aurora shrieked. She leapt off the balcony and swooped toward him.

Aurora began to frantically prod Nautilus. "What in Elementa happened to you?" she demanded. "Are you okay? Say something!"

"Ouch," Nautilus groaned. He weakly batted Aurora's paw away. "Knock it off."

Ember suddenly appeared beside Aurora. His orange eyes were filled with concern as he peered down at Nautilus. "For the moon's sake," he growled. "Is this the new thing? Every time one of us goes on an adventure, our snout gets wounded! First it happened to Aurora when she fought Sandstorm. Now it's happened to you!" Ember pointed a claw at Nautilus' nose. "What caused this? You look awful, Nautilus."

"Gee, thanks," he retorted.

Aurora gently placed her paw on Nautilus'. Jealousy filled Ember's entire face, but the others didn't notice. "Tell us what happened," Aurora kindly told Nautilus. "Please. We're worried about you. Did someone attack you? Is there some type of danger in the Water Pack?"

Nautilus covered his eyes with his paws, like he always used to do as a pup. "It was awful," he groaned. "I messed up so badly, and I didn't even realize it until it was too late."

Nautilus wasn't sure why he was speaking so openly about his trauma, but he didn't stop himself. "They saw my mistakes. They could tell that I didn't belong. There was so much whispering. I was terrified. I began to swim. I started to cry. My vision. I didn't see him." Nautilus' voice trembled. "The chariot hit me, knocking me out. There was blood everywhere when I woke up. Prince Benthos threatened me, so I fled."

Nautilus moved his paws aside. He looked up at Aurora and Ember pleadingly. "I can't go back," he choked out. "Never. I'm not safe in the Water Pack Empire anymore. Don't make me go back. Please. I'm begging you."

Aurora and Ember exchanged an unnerved look.

"I know you wanted me to unite the Water Pack with the Sky Pack, and eventually help unify all four packs, but I can't do it." Nautilus couldn't hold back his tears. They streaked down his face. "I told you earlier that I'm not fit to be a part of your group, and you didn't listen to me. Do you believe me now?"

"You belong with us," Aurora instantly responded, defiance filling her voice.

Both wolves turned to look at Ember, who had remained silent and unmoving for most of the conversation. Ember didn't flinch at their gazes. "I told you once, and I'll tell you again," he calmly told Nautilus. "It's not the end of the world if you mess up in the Water Pack." Ember didn't say another word after that. Instead, he gave Nautilus a meaningful look.

It's not the end of the world, because I have the Fire Pack to turn to, Nautilus remembered. His heartbeat quickened. *I can leave Nautilus behind forever, and become Singe the Fire Wolf.*

A hint of satisfaction crept over Ember's face. He must have realized that Nautilus had caught on to what he was suggesting, because he looked away breezily right after.

Aurora's confused gaze flickered between Nautilus and Ember. However, she didn't question her friends. Instead, Aurora extended a paw to help Nautilus stand. She supported him on her shoulder and gently led him toward the bonfire.

Ember watched them go without moving. He then prowled off into the jungle, his ears flattened and his fur bristling. Only Nautilus had seen the murderous glint in Ember's eyes. *Oh no,* he thought queasily. *I hope he doesn't think that I'm trying to steal Aurora's attention from him. He'll probably rip my fur off while I'm asleep or something!*

Nautilus immediately stepped away from Aurora. "I'm all right on my own," he spluttered loudly, hoping that Ember had heard him from wherever he had stalked off to.

Aurora blinked, looking completely weirded out. She then shrugged her shoulders. "Okay," she said nonchalantly. "Anyway. Let's settle down and talk about our next steps later. You've had a long day, Nautilus. I'm sure you must be hungry. Lucky for you, my Jungle Soup Surprise is ready, and it's quite tasty if I do say so myself." The Sky Wolf gave him a cheeky grin, trying to lighten the mood.

Nautilus nodded vigorously, his heart racing.

The hybrid was on edge for the rest of the night. He had choked down his Jungle Soup Surprise quickly, while sitting as far away from Aurora as possible, without looking rude. Ember hadn't returned to the camp for hours, causing Nautilus' stress to rise steadily by the minute. He constantly glanced over his shoulder, expecting Ember to come out of nowhere to bite him.

Ember was always jealous of my powers, Nautilus thought with trembling paws. *What must he think of me now, if he suspects that I'm trying to steal Aurora from him?* Nautilus gulped. Flashes of blood and torn fur exploded through his mind. *No. Ember would never hurt me. Would he?*

Nautilus remembered the time when he, along with Aurora, Ember, and Sandstorm, had been at the Howl Dome in the Earth Pack City. Ember had revealed to his friends that he had been born without an elemental power. Ember had grown angry with Nautilus—that was when his jealousy for the hybrid first showed itself.

Nautilus would never forget the raw hatred in Ember's eyes. The Fire Wolf had taken a menacing step toward him, growling through bared fangs. Nautilus had braced himself for Ember to attack, fearing the worst. Thankfully, Ember had managed to control himself at the last moment, but Nautilus often wondered what he would have done if he hadn't backed off.

"You've been staring at your empty bowl for at least ten minutes," Aurora's voice suddenly joked. "Do you want some more? All you have to do is ask."

Nautilus snapped back to the present. He suddenly realized that he was digging his claws into the stone, bowl-shaped rock he was holding. Nautilus winced, softening his grip. "Oh, no thank you," he replied. "I'm... fine. It was delicious, though."

Aurora was silent for a moment, giving him a quizzical look like he was a riddle she couldn't solve. "All right," she eventually said. "If you say so." The orange light from the bonfire flickered over her white pelt. Aurora rose to her paws and stretched, yawning.

By now, the sky was inky black, and shimmered with countless stars. The moon brightly shone on the island, turning the exotic trees silver. Crickets chirped rhythmically, filling the silence with their song.

Ember was still nowhere to be seen.

Aurora yawned again. "I'm going to sleep," she announced groggily. Her green eyes brightened as a thought came to her. Nautilus winced when she moved closer to him. "Hey! I have the best idea. Why don't you spend the night with Ember and I in the treehouse? There's enough room for all three of us."

"No!" Nautilus shouted in alarm.

Aurora looked startled.

Nautilus' cheeks burned with embarrassment. "I mean, no thank you. Sorry. I'm okay on the ground. The grass is surprisingly soft, and, uh, it's nice to sleep under the sky." Nautilus gave her a nervous smile.

Aurora shrugged. "Whatever works best for you," she responded. "If you see Ember, tell him I'll go fishing in the morning. Good night, Nautilus." Aurora turned around and leapt into the air. She landed on the treehouse's balcony, then disappeared inside.

Nautilus gulped. He suddenly felt more alone than ever before. Nautilus turned around in a full circle, scanning the area for Ember. *Has he been waiting for Aurora to leave me alone?* he wondered with a pounding heart. *Will he strike now, because she isn't here to protect me anymore?*

Nautilus was violently shaking from ears to tail. He slowly lifted up one of his paws to look at the bracelet on his wrist. *You need to stop overacting, Nautilus,* he scolded himself. *Don't you remember what Aurora told you?* He released a shuddering breath. *Ember crafted this bracelet by paw, wanting to surprise me with a gift. He worked hard to make me happy.*

Unless it was all just a trick, a part of Nautilus whispered.

He gave his head a shake, as if he could fling away his troubling thoughts. Nautilus silently crept to the far side of the meadow, wincing whenever his paws accidentally snapped a twig. With eyes as wide as an owl, he slowly lowered himself to the ground, then curled up into a tight ball of fur.

Unsurprisingly, Nautilus couldn't sleep. He stared into the distance without blinking, keeping his ears perked for the first sign of Ember's approach. *Where in Elementa has he gone?* Nautilus wondered. *He can't be that angry, can he? It's not like I asked Aurora to be friendly with me. She wasn't even acting out of the ordinary! Aurora is kind to everyone, not just me. If Ember honestly thinks that she likes me, or that I like her, then he must have kelp in his brain!*

Eventually, Nautilus' thoughts began to shift back to the Water Pack Empire. He vividly remembered the faces of every wolf who had stared at him. Their whispering and mockery crept through his brain, replaying over and over again. Nautilus' nose began to sting when he remembered the zooming chariot. He could practically feel Prince Benthos' cold claws as he snagged them into his fur.

Nautilus' head began to swirl with a tornado of anxious thoughts. His worries about Ember, and his embarrassment surrounding the Water Pack Empire, quickly grew to be overwhelming. Nautilus felt sick. He wanted to dive into the ocean and swim far away from Elementa altogether.

Why did I ever allow myself to be caught up in my friends' journey? he wondered in despair. *I was a fool to think that coming out of my shell was a good idea. I should have stayed separated from the rest of the world. I should have never ventured into The Hidden Howl. I should have never invited Aurora and Ember into my life. Everything went wrong the moment I started interacting with other wolves!*

Nautilus' jaw clenched. *Why should I bother becoming a Fire Wolf?* he wondered. *I don't belong with them any more than I belong with the Water Pack. I'll mess up there, too.* Nautilus' eyes narrowed. *No. What I need is no pack, no friends, and no wolves to disappoint. I made the mistake of opening up to the world. It's time I fix that mistake. Being a lone wolf is who I'm supposed to be.*

Nautilus inhaled a deep breath. He then rose to his paws and silently crept toward the ocean. *I can't go back to my den on the beach,* Nautilus realized. *That will be the first place Aurora and Ember look when they realize I'm gone. Maybe I'll find an island far beyond Elementa. A place that I can truly call home.*

Nautilus silently walked through the jungle. Fireflies illuminated the night as they floated above his head. Before long, Nautilus arrived at the shore. He hesitated, his heart twisting with grief. *Maybe I'm overreacting,* Nautilus thought. *I'm definitely not Ember's favourite wolf, but is it fair to think he might hurt me... or worse? What about Aurora? She'll be heartbroken once she realizes I'm gone. She'll probably blame herself for something that she didn't do.*

Aren't Aurora, Ember and I a team? Didn't we face and defeat Queen Tempest together? Haven't they treated me like I'm family, when nobody else has?

Nautilus' ears flattened. He was motionless for a long time. *I can't continue being afraid all the time,* he told himself. *This is my life to live, and my decision to make. I don't belong with the Water Pack or the Fire Pack, and if I'm being honest, I've never belonged with Aurora, Ember, or Sandstorm either. They'd be better off without me. This is for their benefit, too.*

Nautilus quietly walked toward the ocean. The waves crashed against the shore, causing salty droplets to hit his face. Nautilus prepared himself to leave Emora Island for good. Then—

"Nautilus!" a voice shouted. "Wait!"

Nautilus whirled around, his paws slipping on the wet sand. He let out a yelp. It was Ember—and he was running straight toward him.

Great, Nautilus thought, somehow managing to feel sarcastic moments before he got torn to shreds. *Of course he's trying to stop me. That's just my luck.*

Nautilus, even to his surprise, bared his fangs and snarled. "Back off," he hissed to Ember. "You don't need to worry about me anymore. I'm leaving. It'll just be you and Aurora now."

Ember was so startled by Nautilus' words that he skidded to a halt. "What in Elementa are you talking about?" he snapped. "Just me and Aurora? What's that supposed to mean?"

Nautilus blinked. "Aren't you..." he trailed off, feeling suddenly embarrassed.

Ember's orange eyes widened. "Aren't I what?" he demanded grouchily.

Nautilus nervously fiddled with the fins on his tail. "You know," he stammered. "Trying to, uh, kill me for being close with Aurora?"

Ember was so shocked that he couldn't speak for a moment. "WHAT?!" he roared. "Kill you? Have you lost your mind? Why would I ever do that?! I might claw you for saying something so dumb, though!"

Nautilus felt embarrassed, relieved, and nervous all at once. "I saw the look on your face when Aurora walked beside me," he stammered. "You were furious."

Ember growled. "Well, of course I was," he spat. "I love Aurora. She makes me happy. Before I met her, my life was miserable and lonely. I was so desperate for friends that I wandered into that dopey Hidden Howl just so I wouldn't be alone."

Nautilus' eyes widened. "That's exactly why I joined The Hidden Howl," he confessed.

Ember gritted his teeth, looking beyond embarrassed. "Whatever," he grumbled. "My point is, I care about Aurora a lot, and I won't deny that I'm a bit overprotective of her. Did you really think that I would attack you over something so petty, though?"

Nautilus couldn't meet Ember's gaze. He nodded while staring at the ground.

Ember let out an angry growl. "Gee," he huffed. "Thanks a lot."

Nautilus lifted his head defensively. "How was I supposed to know?" he demanded. "You freaked me out, Ember. You stalked off with the most jealous look on your face, then disappeared for hours. How was I *not* supposed to be worried?" Nautilus frowned. "Where were you all that time, anyway?"

Now it was Ember who looked awkward. "I was, uh, watching you," he confessed in a small voice.

Nautilus' fur bristled. "Excuse me?" he squealed.

Ember kicked at a loose pebble, sending it flying across the beach. "You freaked me out too, Nautilus," he said. "I got angry when you talked about abandoning Aurora and I again That wasn't what bothered me the most, though. I realized that I probably shouldn't have suggested that you live in the Fire Pack." Ember frowned. "You seemed so worried and scared about the Water Pack. After being rattled like that, I thought for sure that you would do something foolish. So, I watched you all night, waiting to see what you would do in secret."

Ember's eyes were bright with anger. "And it's a good thing that I did," he snarled. "I knew you would run away! Where are you planning to go, Nautilus? The Fire Pack? Trust me, that's the last place you want to be. I regret that I ever told you to live there."

Nautilus frowned. "I was planning on leaving Elementa altogether, actually," he mumbled. "I don't belong here."

Ember rolled his eyes. "Oh, please," he scoffed. "Are you back to feeling sorry for yourself? What, you think that just because you made some mistakes that it's game over? Pick yourself back up, shake the dust off your pelt, and try again. Every wolf has messed up in life, and every wolf struggles with something. You're not the only one with problems."

Nautilus didn't respond.

Ember dug his claws into the sand underfoot. "I'm not going to let you give up," he snarled. "Your fear isn't going to consume you. Not on my watch. You're going back to the Water Pack Empire tomorrow morning, and you're going to show those wolves who's boss. Prove that they're wrong about you."

Nautilus shrunk in his own fur. "You're not going to let me get out of this, are you?" he mumbled.

Ember smirked. "You know that I'm not," he responded gruffly. "Now, will you please go to sleep? Quit worrying so much. Since you know that I'm *not* trying to kill you, you'll hopefully get a good rest. Yes?" Irritation glimmered in his orange eyes.

"Yes," Nautilus sighed. "Sorry again about that." He fiddled with the bracelet on his wrist, feeling comforted by the smooth bark as it slid across his fur. Nautilus kept his head low as he followed Ember through the jungle, and into the meadow.

Nautilus flopped to the ground with a dramatic sigh, feeling as blobby as a jellyfish. He closed his eyes, even though he knew that sleep wasn't going to come easily tonight. *At least things can't get any worse from here,* Nautilus thought.

Little did he realize that things were going to get a whole lot worse.

CHAPTER 8

Returning here was a mistake, Nautilus inwardly groaned. He felt the eyes of the Water Pack Empire on him as he swam through the streets in silence. Nautilus had never felt so nervous and out of place in all his life. *If the Water Wolves think badly of me now, how will they react if they ever find out that I'm a hybrid?* He nearly fainted at the thought.

Whenever Nautilus swam too close to someone, they immediately bolted out of the way, as if he had some type of infectious disease. "I've heard that he's a runaway from the Outer Islands," a wolf gossiped, just loud enough for Nautilus to overhear.

"That would explain a lot," her friend murmured. He stared at Nautilus with cold eyes. "If he is an islander, he should've known better than to come here." Nautilus shuddered at the threat in his voice. Whatever an 'islander' was, it clearly wasn't welcome in the underwater empire.

Nautilus nearly wailed with despair. *What is wrong with me?!* he wondered fearfully. *Why did I ever agree to come back here? After what happened with Prince Benthos, I should've been smart enough to stay clear of this place. It was a mistake to listen to Ember. I should have swum away from Elementa this morning, when I had a chance.*

Nautilus had almost done just that, after he had plunged into the ocean near Emora Island. Before he could pick a direction, and swim away from Elementa forever, Nautilus had glanced at his bracelet. The sight filled him with guilt, reminding him that he couldn't abandon his friends, despite how much he was tempted to.

Although it was beyond awful, Nautilus knew in his heart that returning to the Water Pack Empire was the right thing to do. *I can tell that my destiny will be fulfilled here,* he thought with a clenched jaw. *Whether I like it or not, the empire is where I need to be.*

Without warning, two massive guards appeared out of nowhere. They halted right in front of Nautilus, pointing their frightening tridents at him. Nautilus squealed like a pup.

"You have been summoned by Prince Benthos," one of the guards growled. "Come with us quietly. Do not resist."

Nautilus' eyes wildly darted around as he tried to locate some means of escape. *I need to get out of here!* he thought in panic.

Before Nautilus could bolt away, one of the guards dangerously moved her trident closer, growling fiercely. "I said, *do not resist.*" Her amber eyes were locked on Nautilus, like he was prey and she was a predator. Her pale blue fur was streaked with silver stripes, and she carried many scars. The guard didn't have a fish-like tail. Her only aquatic features were gills, and powerful webs between each of her claws. Nautilus could tell that this wolf was fast... and certainly no stranger to violence. "Trust me," she hissed. "Trying anything will only end badly for you."

Nautilus nodded vigorously. "I understand," he spluttered. "Please don't hurt me."

She stared at him for a long moment, her amber eyes shining dangerously. Then, she turned to face the second guard. "Cuff his paws," she ordered.

"Yes, Commander Wave," he replied automatically. Before Nautilus could even flinch, the guard seized his front paws and shackled them together. Fear thundered through Nautilus' veins when Commander Wave leaned forward to peer at the bracelet on his wrist. Luckily, she didn't question Nautilus' fashion choices, and merely gave him a suspicious glare.

The second guard roughly pushed Nautilus forward. Commander Wave led the way to the royal castle, while Nautilus and the guard followed closely behind her.

Nautilus' heart was beating so violently that he thought it would burst out of his chest. *Ember's going to get it if I make it out of this alive!* he thought, half frustrated and half mortified. *This is all his fault. He made me come back here! I shouldn't have listened. Why did I do it? Why?!*

"What are my charges?" Nautilus abruptly blurted. "What did I do wrong? I didn't hurt anyone. I didn't steal or trespass, either. All I did was get hit by a chariot by *accident*! I think you've got the wrong wolf."

Commander Wave suddenly halted. Nautilus stiffened, immediately regretting how he'd spoken out. Wave looked over her shoulder to glance at Nautilus. To his surprise, there wasn't any rage in her striking amber eyes. "Prince Benthos was very clear that you're the wolf he wants to see," Wave explained in a professionally calm voice. "You're suspected of being a runaway from the Outer Islands."

"What does that even mean?!" Nautilus protested.

"Silence," Wave snarled, not wanting him to think he could speak openly whenever he pleased. "Prince Benthos will explain everything." Without giving Nautilus a chance to respond, Wave looked away and continued swimming.

This is a nightmare, Nautilus thought pitifully. As he was ushered into the royal castle, he couldn't help but wonder if he'd ever see the light of day again. His anxiety was made especially worse when Wave led him toward a dark tunnel that reached below the ocean floor. *An underground cellar,* Nautilus realized queasily. *Can this day get any worse?*

"Wait for us here," Wave ordered the second guard, who halted immediately. Wave then escorted Nautilus down into the shadowy passage.

Glowing moss illuminated the darkness with a sickly shade of blue. They grew on the roof of the tunnel, swaying eerily when the Water Wolves swam by. Nautilus gagged when he spotted fish bones littered throughout the area.

After what felt like hours, Wave and Nautilus reached the end of the tunnel. There was a single door waiting for them. It looked ancient, and had rusted significantly after so many years underwater. Nautilus gave Wave a fearful glance. To his absolute shock, she gave him a sympathetic look. "You'll be fine," Wave said, not gently, but not unkindly either. She quickly glanced at the shut door, then whispered, "Just a word of advice. Speak as little as possible around Benthos. He'll pounce on every word you say to twist its meaning."

Nautilus' eyes widened. Why in Elementa was Wave helping him? Before he could utter a word, Wave suddenly opened the squeaky door and pushed him into the room. Wave shut the door immediately, sealing Nautilus inside.

The room was empty, aside from a stone table and two chairs. One was occupied by Prince Benthos himself. He looked just as unfriendly as the last time Nautilus had seen him. Benthos' yellow eyes were narrowed, and his shark-like tail was raised dangerously, making him look bigger than he actually was. "Have a seat," Benthos demanded in a venomous voice.

Left with no choice, Nautilus reluctantly sat on the seat opposite of Benthos.

The room was painfully silent for a long, long moment. No wolf moved.

"If I remember correctly," Benthos eventually growled, "your name is Nautilus. Is that right?" Benthos' steel-blue fur began to rise.

Nautilus nodded. He didn't dare speak, remembering Wave's advice.

Benthos slowly leaned forward. "You've created quite a stir these last couple of days," he told Nautilus. "Why is that?"

Nautilus paused, thinking carefully about his response. *Benthos is trying to make me say something that he can use against me,* Nautilus realized. Perhaps, in a situation like this, the best response was no response at all. Nautilus said nothing.

Benthos clasped his webbed paws together, frustration shining in his yellow eyes. "I've been dying to learn some more about you," he continued in a voice as sharp as daggers. "My apologies if this comes off as rude, Nautilus, but I can't help noticing how... different... you seem. It's almost as if you don't belong here."

The pause that followed was excruciating. Nautilus' paws started to tremble. Luckily, the table hid them from Benthos' sight.

"A strange wolf like you is not common here in my empire," Benthos said in a slithering voice. "If I've heard the stories correctly, you needed lessons on how to speak from a kindergarten class. You also invaded a pet shop, almost eating the unfortunate fish inside. Then, you entered *my* castle and broke *my* Silent Hour Policy."

"Silent Hour Policy?" Nautilus choked out.

Benthos' eyes brightened, as if he had successfully pounced on his prey. "You don't know?" he asked in fake surprise. "Why, everyone in the empire knows about the Silent Hour Policy. Everyone that *belongs* in the empire, anyway."

"What's the policy for?" Nautilus asked, not falling into Benthos' trap.

Benthos let out a slow, condescending laugh. "My," he said. "You truly are clueless to how things work around here. Don't you know that I *own* the Water Pack Empire?"

"You're only a prince," Nautilus growled, with much more hostility than he had intended.

Benthos smirked. "A prince that will soon become king," he corrected. "As such, I set the rules. I make the polices. I tell wolves what they can and cannot do. That's where my brilliant Silent Hour Policy comes in. My subjects need to know who's in control. I can't let them think that they're equal to me, can I?"

Benthos' jagged ears flattened. "What they need to learn is obedience. I'm starting to train them with small, simple steps. First, it's no talking in the castle when I tell them. Then, it'll be something bigger, like the best portions of prey go to me only. Next, I think I'll implement something grand, like every wolf in the empire must do work that benefits me alone. Doesn't that sound marvelous?"

"Nightmarish is more like it," Nautilus snapped without thinking. "You don't sound like a leader. You sound like a dictator."

Benthos shrugged. "You can call it that," he chuckled. "It makes no difference to me."

"Does the empire know about your selfishness?" Nautilus demanded fiercely. Why was he getting so angry, and so protective of the Water Pack? It wasn't like him to get this passionate about something. "Are they aware of what you plan to do to them?"

Benthos let out a sneering laugh. "Of course not," he replied. "Nobody knows. I can't have an uprising on my paws, can I?"

Nautilus' flanks rose and fell with every sharp breath he took. "What makes you think that I'm not going to expose you?" he asked. Nautilus immediately regretted hearing the answer to his question.

Benthos smiled. "Because you'll be dead within the hour," he replied matter-of-factly.

Nautilus' eyes widened. Fear flooded his veins like a tsunami. "What?" he choked out.

"Dead," Benthos repeated. "Gone. Never to be seen again. Oh, don't look so surprised. You must have seen this coming. I hate to be so blunt, but nobody in the Water Pack likes you, Nautilus. You have caused my citizens unrest. They're worried about even more outsiders invading the empire, thanks to you. I need to give them peace of mind. They need to see that their beloved prince doesn't tolerate unwelcomed guests from the Outer Islands."

Something inside Nautilus snapped. "I don't even know what the Outer Islands are!" he screamed.

Benthos examined his claws with a bored expression on his face. "Acting clueless won't help your situation," he scoffed. "But if you insist on a recap, the Outer Islands are where we send the wolves that nobody likes. They're banished from the empire forever once they end up there. Even their offspring, and the next generation of islanders, aren't allowed to return. If they do happen to be foolish enough to come back, the consequence is a public execution." Benthos looked up and gave Nautilus a meaningful stare.

"I'm not from the Outer Islands," Nautilus spluttered. "At least, I don't think that I am." Nautilus immediately slapped a paw over his mouth, regretting his choice of words immediately. "Wait! No. Uh, forget that I said that."

"Excuse me?" Benthos growled. He abruptly stood up, looming over Nautilus. "If you're not an islander, or a descendant of one, then what are you?"

Nautilus' heartbeat quickened. "I'm a Water Wolf," he choked out. *If he finds out that I'm a hybrid, he'll finish me off on the spot.*

Benthos slammed his fists on the table. "No you're not," he hissed. "No Water Wolf is this pathetic. Not even the islanders are this bad. I should have suspected that there was something more going on from the start." Benthos bared his razor-sharp fangs. "Who. Are. You. Answer me!"

Nautilus flinched away from Benthos. "I already told you!" he screamed back. "I'm Nautilus the Water Wolf!"

Benthos abruptly seized the fur near Nautilus' neck, then lifted him off the chair. "I don't know who—or what—you are," Benthos rumbled. "But I know that one thing is clear. You don't belong in my ocean." Benthos lifted his other paw, ready to land the finishing blow.

"Wave!" Nautilus screamed. "Help!"

Commander Wave abruptly burst into the room, her eyes wide. "I heard screaming," she panted. Wave froze when she caught sight of Nautilus and Benthos. "What is going on here?!"

Benthos flashed her a toothy grin. "I'm just dealing with this prisoner," he huffed.

"By harming him?" Wave demanded. "Or were you planning on doing worse?"

Benthos' eyes narrowed into furious slits. "Don't you dare question your prince," he spat. "Know your place."

Wave, to Nautilus' shock, pulled back her lips and snarled. "Know yours, first," she retorted dangerously. "Only the pack leader is allowed to decide the fate of prisoners. Now. Let him go." Wave's webbed paws gripped her trident harder, as if she was preparing herself to attack Benthos.

Benthos glowered at Nautilus. "This is far from over," he whispered into his ear. Benthos roughly pushed Nautilus away from him, sending him floundering across the room.

Nautilus swam over to Wave and hid behind her, using her like a shield. Wave glared at Benthos for a few moments, before turning her head to give Nautilus an unhappy look. "Come with me," she sighed, nudging him toward the door. "King Delta will decide your fate."

The cuffs around Nautilus' paws felt as tight as ever. He swam beside Wave in silence, feeling dizzy. Benthos followed closely behind, glaring at Nautilus without ceasing. *If King Delta's son is this awful,* Nautilus thought, *how much worse will he be?* Nautilus shuddered. He could only hope that King Delta was in a merciful mood today.

CHAPTER 9

Nautilus was fairly certain that they had been swimming for at least an eternity. He gasped and wheezed, trying to catch his breath. "Are we almost there?" Nautilus groaned to Wave. "I'm exhausted. How much further do we have to go?"

They had swum through corridor after corridor, and still hadn't reached their destination. It felt like the colossal castle went on forever.

Wave, who was continuing to lead the group, shrugged nonchalantly. "King Delta's throne room isn't much further," she replied, without turning around.

Nautilus frowned unhappily. The pressure of the pawcuffs were making his wrists sore, and their weight caused him to swim lopsidedly. "The sooner we get there, the better," Nautilus huffed. His words were followed by a long silence.

Suddenly, Benthos swam closer to Nautilus, flashing him a wicked grin. "I'm surprised," he murmured in a voice so quiet that only Nautilus could hear. "You appear to be in a hurry to meet my father."

Nautilus met his gaze. "Not really," he said, before Benthos could continue his monologue. "I'm just sick of swimming. Do you think these cuffs are really necessary? You're acting like I'm some type of threat to you." Nautilus smiled with fake innocence, knowing that he'd struck a nerve.

Frustration spilled over Benthos' face. "I'll admit my faults," he grumbled. "It was a mistake to tell you my plans for the empire. However, in my defense, I hadn't expected you to cry out to Wave like a complete coward. You should have been fed to the sharks right about now." Benthos gave Nautilus a seething glare. "No, you won't be a threat. Father will finish what I started and get rid of you." Benthos dangerously lowered his voice. "And if he doesn't destroy you, I'll personally see to it myself."

Benthos drifted behind Nautilus like a dark shadow, watching his every move. It made Nautilus' pelt itch uncomfortably. *Well,* he thought with a gulp. *That was completely terrible.* Regret made him feel sick. *I can't believe that things have gone so wrong, so soon. If I'd known that I would be meeting the king of the Water Pack in chains, I would've never shown my face in the empire.* Nautilus sighed. *I should have listened to my instincts from the start. I'm not cut out for big heroic missions. If only I stayed home. I could have prevented all of this.*

Wave came to a sudden halt. "We've arrived," she announced.

Nautilus was immediately snapped out of his troubling thoughts. His green eyes widened.

They had reached a set of two enormous, pearly white doors. Tiny flecks of silver were imprinted into the smooth surfaces, decorating them from top to bottom. Nautilus' heart began to race, knowing that King Delta was just on the other side of this doorway.

Nautilus felt a sudden sensation of vertigo, like he was falling backward. "I think I'm going to be sick," Nautilus groaned. "I just... need a minute." He woozily sunk to the floor in a heap of dark blue fur.

Wave nodded with an emotionless expression. However, Benthos immediately snatched Nautilus' scruff with his claws. He threw the doors open and roughly dragged Nautilus into the room. "Hello, Father!" Benthos greeted with a mocking sneer. "I have a wolf that I'm just *dying* for you to meet." Benthos kicked Nautilus, sending him floundering forward.

Before Nautilus could steady himself, he bumped right against the base of King Delta's golden throne. Nautilus slowly looked up, trembling violently.

Staring down at him was King Delta himself. His pale green eyes were filled with curiosity, while his light blue fur shone magnificently in the sunlight. King Delta wore a dazzling crown, and two matching armbands. Nautilus froze, realizing that his accessories were imprinted with tiny blue crystals.

King Delta is wearing Blue Elemental Heart! he thought. *But why? Queen Tempest had used White Elemental Heart to build a superweapon. Is King Delta planning on doing the same?*

King Delta's ears flattened.

Nautilus nearly fainted. He'd been staring at the king without even realizing it. How humiliating! From the sidelines, Benthos smirked, enjoying Nautilus' embarrassment.

"Prince Benthos," King Delta suddenly demanded, turning his attention onto his son. "What is the meaning of this? Why has this wolf been brought to me?" King Delta swished his fish-like tail forward to neatly wrap it around his paws.

Nautilus shuffled away from the throne. His heart was beating so fiercely that he thought the entire empire could hear it. Nautilus' breathing quickened. *No! I can't hyperventilate now! Not in front of King Delta. Calm down, Nautilus. Calm down!* Nautilus gritted his teeth.

Benthos swam forward, looking pleased. "This wolf has slithered into our ocean when he doesn't belong among us," he announced, while pointing a paw at Nautilus. "I was planning on dealing with him myself, but alas, our dear Commander Wave insisted that I present the traitor to you first."

Benthos looked over his shoulder to give Wave an angry glare.

King Delta appeared less than impressed. "I'm glad you listened to her," he replied calmly. "Only the pack leader is allowed to decide the fate of prisoners."

Without warning, King Delta broke off into a brutal coughing fit. Bubbles exploded out of his mouth and tumbled throughout the room.

Nautilus flinched. He was tempted to ask if King Delta was all right, but didn't dare speak. It wasn't his place to talk right now.

Once King Delta recovered, Benthos clasped his front paws together. "Yes, of course," he replied with a hint of venom in his voice. "But as I'm sure you recall, Father, I'll soon be king. As such, I figured bothering you with this lowly worm was less than necessary." Benthos gave the king a smile that was all teeth.

King Delta nodded dismissively at Benthos, then turned his head to gaze at Nautilus. "Where have you come from?" he asked. "Are my son's accusations about you true? You have my permission to speak."

Nautilus bowed instinctively. "Thank you, Your Highness," he spluttered. "What Prince Benthos says is false. I'm not from the Outer Islands."

King Delta leaned forward. "Where are you from, then?" he asked curiously. "What part of the empire do you call home?"

Nautilus froze. "Uh," he stammered. "I, uh..."

Benthos crossed his arms, grinning wickedly. Wave raised an eyebrow. King Delta continued to stare at Nautilus without blinking. This was really, really bad.

Nautilus anxiously fiddled with the fins on his tail. *I had no idea they labelled parts of the empire!* he thought. *How am I supposed to answer that? Should I say I'm from Water Way? Seashell Shores? King Delta will definitely know that I'm an outsider if I can't even name a real sector of the empire. Is there any point in lying to him?*

King Delta lashed his fish-like tail impatiently. "Well?" he asked. "I don't have all day. What part of the empire are you from?"

Nautilus looked down at his paws, unable to meet the king's gaze. "The truth is," he choked out, "I'm not from the Water Pack Empire." Nautilus winced, expecting an explosion of gasps, questions, and accusations. However, not a single wolf spoke. A deafening silence filled the throne room for a long moment.

Benthos studied his claws with a bored expression. "That's no surprise, is it?" he sneered. "It was obvious that you're not one of us. My question is this: if you're not an islander, then what are you? Or, more interestingly, who are you?"

King Delta grimaced. "Answer the prince's question," he told Nautilus. Was there a hint of desperation in King Delta's voice, or had Nautilus just imagined it?

Nautilus' gills fluttered rapidly. His chest felt tight, making it a struggle to breathe. *They can't know that I'm a hybrid,* he told himself in a panic. *Absolutely nobody can know. I won't tell them the truth, but I won't lie to them, either.* Nautilus' paws started to tremble.

"The truth is, I'm not a real citizen of the Water Pack Empire," he confessed. "I had never entered the ocean's depths until a few days ago. I was abandoned by my parents when I was born, and grew up alone for many, many moons. I raised myself on the shores of Elementa, and never dared to go near any of the elemental packs. But, recently, I decided that I wanted to go home. I wanted to return to the Water Pack."

Nautilus released a shuddering breath. "I know that I'm strange," he continued. "I know that I don't belong here, and that I've made mistakes. But I'm not an Islander. I'm not a threat to you or anyone." Nautilus gave King Delta a pleading look. "Please don't punish me. I'll leave you and the empire forever if that's what you wish, and you'll never see me again. Just... please have mercy on me. Don't let Benthos have his way. I don't deserve what he has planned."

Benthos' eyes narrowed into furious slits.

King Delta paused for a moment, considering Nautilus' plea. There was no emotion in his eyes. His face didn't reveal a trace of what he was thinking.

Nautilus held his breath, adrenaline thundering through his veins. Then—

"I pardon you in full," King Delta announced. "You will not receive punishment. I deem you to be innocent."

Benthos' face twisted with rage. Wave smiled.

Nautilus was so relieved that he nearly fainted. "Thank you, Your Highness," he breathed. "I really appreciate it."

King Delta gave Nautilus a nod of acknowledgement. "You may also stay in the empire if you wish," he said. "I see no reason why you can't rejoin your pack."

After so many embarrassments and hardships, Nautilus wasn't sure how he felt about living in the underwater empire anymore. So, Nautilus responded with a simple "thank you", not wanting to seem ungrateful. "Am I free to go?" he asked.

King Delta shifted his paws, looking unexpectedly nervous. What had come over the king? "Yes," he responded slowly, "but I'd like to ask you one more thing before you leave. There's something that I need to know about you."

Nautilus shuddered involuntarily. "Okay," he murmured. "What is it, Your Majesty?"

King Delta looked nervous, confused, and hopeful all at once. Silence fell over the room. Nobody moved. "Are you..." King Delta hesitated. It appeared to be a struggle to choke out the words. "Are you... half Fire Wolf?"

Every muscle in Nautilus' body froze. His blood seemed to turn to ice. Fear oozed over him, while despair seized his heart. "What?" Nautilus whimpered.

King Delta looked just as anguished as Nautilus felt. "Half Fire Wolf," he repeated, desperately trying to keep his voice from shaking. "Are you a hybrid? Don't you dare lie to me! I need to know. I need to know if you're *him*. Please. Tell me the truth."

Nautilus backed away, his heart racing. "I don't know what you're talking about," he stammered. "I'm a Water Wolf. I'm not... it's not... I'm..." Before Nautilus could stop himself, he turned tail and bolted. Nautilus swam toward the door like his life depended on it. Nautilus needed to get out of here. King Delta *knew*. A wolf knew his secret! How did he know?!

Just before Nautilus could escape, Wave tackled Nautilus and pinned him to the ground. "The king asked you a question," she snarled. "Answer him immediately!"

"Wave, stop," King Delta gasped. "Don't hurt him."

Wave's amber eyes widened. "Why?" she asked, absolutely stunned.

Joy filled King Delta's face. "Because this wolf is my son," he whispered. "The true heir to the throne has returned at last."

CHAPTER 10

"What?!" Nautilus squealed.

"I beg your pardon?!" Benthos screamed at the same time. His steel-blue fur wildly bristled, making the already giant wolf look twice his size. Rage lit up his yellow eyes. "True heir to the throne? I am the only true heir to the throne! I'm Prince Benthos! I'm the wolf who will become king!" Benthos whipped around to glare at Nautilus. "There will be no challenger to my reign. Especially when that challenger is an abomination hybrid!"

Nautilus' gaze darted between King Delta and Benthos. Was this some type of feverish nightmare? These wolves—who were royalty, no less—were his family? No. It couldn't be true. It just couldn't be. How could a wolf like Benthos possibly be Nautilus' brother? They were nothing alike. King Delta must be mistaken. However, before Nautilus could doubt the Water Pack leader any further, King Delta wrapped his arms around his son.

Nautilus froze in sheer panic, unsure of what to do. It took him a few moments to realize what King Delta was doing. It wasn't an attack, like his first guess had been. King Delta, his father, was hugging him. This was amazing. Nautilus felt safe and comforted, like there was nothing in the world to worry about anymore.

King Delta moved away from Nautilus, giving him a weak smile. "It's really you," he breathed, sounding far less stern and regal than before. Delta took off his crown and held it to his chest. "I can tell that you're my son. You have Ash's kind eyes, and your tail looks just like mine. You're really him. My brave little Nautilus, all grown up." Delta wiped away a tear from his eye.

Benthos, who was watching the scene from the sidelines, looked murderous. Bubbles tumbled out of his nose as he breathed furiously. "This coward is not your son!" Benthos screamed venomously. "I am your son!"

King Delta gave Benthos a sympathetic look. "Adopted son," he said gently. "You already know that I'm not your biological father."

Benthos gritted his teeth lividly. "Let me guess," he fumed. "I've only been a substitute all these years. You took me in because you wanted a replacement for *him*." Benthos' webbed paws curled into fists. "Was I just keeping his seat warm all these years? Were you always secretly hoping for his return, so I wouldn't become king?"

King Delta looked guilty. "I won't deny that I needed an heir to the throne, in case Nautilus never returned," he replied awkwardly. "I've known for years that my days are coming to an end. Benthos, you can't possibly blame me for wanting to secure the future of the Water Pack, especially when my time is so limited." As if on cue, King Delta broke off into another sickly coughing fit.

Nautilus flinched away from his father. "Are you all right?" he asked.

"I'll live for now," King Delta groaned, once he'd recovered. "Don't worry about getting sick yourself, Son. It's not contagious."

Benthos barged in between Delta and Nautilus. "So what you're saying is, I *have* just been a replacement," he growled, refusing to let the topic go. "Who will you give the throne to, Father? The wolf who has loyally served the Water Pack for years, or your new son that randomly showed up one day and made a complete fool of himself?"

King Delta nervously fiddled with the fins on his tail, an anxious habit Nautilus constantly did himself. "Well," King Delta began. "Nautilus *is* my firstborn. It's his birthright to have the throne."

Benthos looked outraged. "So all my training has been for nothing—because of him?" he demanded. "Just look at him! He's younger and smaller than me. It's pathetic!"

Nautilus' fur bristled. "You don't look much older than me," he defensively pointed out. Benthos' glare immediately made him regret speaking. "But, uh, you're definitely bigger than me. And much, err, scarier."

Benthos bared his fangs. "You should be scared of me," he snarled ominously. "You'll regret stealing my throne. I promise it." Without giving his family a chance to respond, Benthos turned around and stormed out the door. He pushed past Wave and slithered out of sight.

King Delta watched Benthos go for a moment, then placed his crown back on his head. He cleared his throat anxiously, breaking the awkward silence that had fallen over the throne room. "Don't worry about your brother," King Delta told Nautilus. "He's always been a bit passionate about leadership, but I'm sure he'll eventually settle down and accept this new reality."

Nautilus gulped. He didn't say it out loud, but he had a terrible feeling that Benthos would do anything but 'settle down'. *Benthos told me information that he'd kill to keep secret,* Nautilus remembered fearfully. *He wasn't planning on me still being alive right now. How far will Benthos go to keep his dictatorship mentality a secret, along with securing the throne all for himself?*

Wave suddenly crept forward, then bowed to King Delta. "Your Highness," she began. "Forgive me for speaking without permission, but there is something that I'd like to ask." Wave looked awkward and determined at the same time. "I mean no offense, but do you truly believe that an heir who is half Fire Wolf can possibly take your place one day? The empire just won't stand for it. They may even turn on you if they find out their king had a relationship with a Fire Wolf. I fear an uprising, especially if Prince Benthos creates division among the pack."

Nautilus nearly fainted. The thought of the entire Water Pack Empire knowing his darkest secret took his breath away. It had been terrifying to reveal his secret to Aurora and Ember. How could he possibly cope with an entire pack knowing?

King Delta sighed. "Your fears are valid," he told Wave. "Unfortunately, not everyone in Elementa is tolerant of the other elementals. I was pleased to hear that Queen Tempest was defeated, and that the Sky Pack is at peace with the world. But there is still a long way to go until all of Elementa is unified." Delta grinned at Nautilus. "Like your mother once said, the rules dividing our packs are 'dumb'. As warfare grows more and more common each day, I agree with her now more than ever."

King Delta clasped his front paws together, looking thoughtful. "We'll keep Nautilus' identity a secret for now," King Delta answered Wave. "I won't let Benthos cause trouble for Nautilus and I. Nobody will know that my son is a hybrid... not until the world is at a better place. For now, we'll tell everyone that Nautilus was simply lost to the empire in an accident as a pup. He's returned to take his place as the rightful ruler of the Water Pack. End of story."

Nautilus felt an explosion of fear. "But I don't want to be the leader of the pack!" he shouted. "I'm not cut out to be a king. Being a leader is not who I am."

Nautilus slowly backed away, his heart racing. "I'm sorry for getting your hopes up," he stammered. "I'm really glad to have met you. But the truth is, I barely know you, and you barely know me. I'm still figuring out how things work in the Water Pack. There's no way I'm ready to be king. Not now. Not ever." Nautilus' paws trembled. "I think it's time I start heading back. It's getting late. My friends must be wondering where I am."

King Delta looked terrified at the thought of losing Nautilus again. "Wait," he said in surprising gentleness. "I'm sorry for pushing the crown on you. Trust me, I know what it feels like to have that happen. Nautilus, I don't expect you to become leader any time soon. I'm sorry if that's what it sounded like." He released a shuddering breath. "I don't want to push you away. I promise that I can be the father you never had. I'll be there for you this time. We can be a family, like we were supposed to be."

Nautilus frowned. "But why did you leave me the first time?" he asked. "I've been wanting to ask you that for years. How come you and my mother abandoned me?"

King Delta's eyes filled with horror. "What do you mean?" he asked. "Not about me abandoning you. About Ash. You mentioned earlier that you had raised yourself for moons, but that wasn't the truth, was it? Your mother was with you the entire time!"

"I wasn't lying," Nautilus said with a hint of bitterness in his voice. "I really did raise myself. Nobody was there for me. What makes you think my mother was with me?"

King Delta looked outraged. "Because my parents promised that if I left you two forever, they would leave you in peace," he hissed. "They lied! I should have known. I bet the moment I returned to the castle, they sent guards back to separate you from Ash." He was so furious that his entire body shook.

Nautilus felt an unexpected wave of sympathy for his father. He'd always assumed that his parents had abandoned him for selfish reasons. Nautilus had never thought that they'd done it because they were left with no other choice. "I'm sorry that happened to you," Nautilus told Delta.

King Delta looked startled. "You aren't... upset?" he asked.

"Of course I'm upset," Nautilus confessed. "I was all alone. I had nobody to turn to. For years I wondered what life could've been like if I had my parents with me. But now I found you. We're together again."

King Delta looked like he was about to cry tears of joy. He gave Nautilus a hug so tight that he thought his bones would snap. "Will you stay?" Delta asked hopefully. "Even just for one night? I promise I won't push any royalty stuff on you."

"Okay," Nautilus wheezed, struggling to breathe in his father's embrace. "I'll stay for the night."

King Delta let Nautilus go. "Wonderful!" he exclaimed. "I'll personally escort you to your room." King Delta swam toward the door with a beaming smile on his face. "Wave, I dismiss you for the night. Follow me, Son."

Nautilus followed closely behind his father, feeling completely weirded out to be called 'son'. Moonlight shone into the long corridors, turning the decorative sculptures silver. Long, eerie shadows were cast throughout the castle, making Nautilus feel nervous. He expected Benthos to be lurking in the dark, ready to attack him at any moment. With a shudder,

Nautilus swam closer to King Delta, feeling safer when he was near.

"Okay," King Delta eventually announced. "Just past this corner... and... here we are! This is your room. It's been waiting for you ever since you were born. And look! Your brother's room is right across from yours. Isn't that great?"

Nautilus felt a stab of fear. How could he possibly sleep knowing that Benthos was right across from him? Perhaps staying here was a mistake. Should Nautilus request a guard to watch over him? What if the guard was in cahoots with Benthos? Before Nautilus could speak, King Delta opened the door and swam into the room. With no other choice, Nautilus followed his father.

A gentle current flowed past the balcony and into the room, causing the kelp curtains to sway. Jars of bioluminescent moss floated through the room like lanterns, softly filling the night with their glow. A clam-shaped bed rested in the corner, and was adorned with fluffy pillows. Nautilus had never used a pillow before. He'd always just used rocks, back in his den on the beach.

"What's all this?" Nautilus asked curiously. On top of Nautilus' bed was a small collection of plush toys. The largest one was of an adorable dolphin.

King Delta looked embarrassed. "Oh, sorry about that," he mumbled. "I made those for you years ago. I, uh, thought you'd come home as a pup. I'll just get them out of your way." King Delta reached out a paw to take away the plush toys.

"Wait," Nautilus said. "Please don't take them. I actually really like them."

King Delta smiled. "The dolphin is named Flippers," he said giddily. "I didn't name the other ones because I wanted you to have the chance to do it. Good night, Son... and welcome home." King Delta closed the door on his way out, leaving Nautilus alone in his brand new room.

Nautilus suddenly felt exhausted. He flopped down on his bed with a dramatic sigh, burying his head in his pillows. *What a day,* he thought. Nautilus scooped up Flippers the dolphin and held it close to his heart. *I can't believe I'm Prince Nautilus now, the potential future king of the Water Pack Empire. With such a big title, how long will it take until I start making enemies?* Nautilus' mind flashed to Benthos. He grimaced. *I've already made one big, terrible, dangerous enemy.*

The question is, how much longer until someone strikes?

CHAPTER 11

Something lightly slithered across Nautilus' shoulders. He blinked open his eyes. *Huh?* he thought, only half awake. *What In Elementa Is going... on... ACK!* Nautilus let out a terrified shriek, floundering backward. He fell off the side of his bed and accidentally turned upside down. Nautilus hurriedly balanced himself. He grabbed a decorative seashell off his desk and pointed it toward his attacker, wielding it like a weapon. Nautilus' paw trembled.

A jellyfish had floated serenely into his room from the open balcony. The morning sunlight shone onto the blobby creature, giving it a golden outline. The jellyfish hovered above Nautilus' bed without moving. If it had eyes, Nautilus had a funny feeling that it'd be staring directly at him. Creepy!

With a shuddering breath, Nautilus placed his seashell back on the side of his desk. He stared at the jellyfish for a few moments, unsure of what to make of it. *At least it's not Benthos out for vengeance,* Nautilus thought shakily. *That would have been an even worse start to the day.*

"Um," Nautilus sheepishly told the jellyfish. "You need to get out. Like, right now. Come on. Shoo. Leave. Err, please?"

The jellyfish didn't budge.

Nautilus slowly crept to his bed, then retrieved Flippers the plush dolphin from underneath the tentacles of the jellyfish. Nautilus moved his paw carefully, trying not to brush against the jellyfish. Of course, despite his best efforts, he touched it anyway. Thankfully, Nautilus' fur blocked all of the jellyfish's sting.

Nautilus gingerly bonked the top of the jellyfish with Flippers, trying to herd the creature out of his room. The jellyfish floated sideways, then immediately glided right back to its spot above Nautilus' bed. He let out a frustrated groan. Nautilus bonked the jellyfish again, and again, and again, but it always ended up floating right back.

"I can't help but think you're doing this on purpose now," Nautilus sniffed at the jellyfish. He fiddled with the fins on his tail. "You can stay here if you want, I guess. There's room for both of us. Just, no touching me when I'm trying to sleep, okay? That was really weird."

The jellyfish didn't respond or move, which made Nautilus feel like a complete fool. "I'm just going to go," he mumbled. Nautilus gave the jellyfish one last uncomfortable look before swimming toward the door. He opened it with a yawn—then yelped.

A wolf was hovering right outside his bedroom, holding a massive trident. Just before Nautilus could faint, he realized that the wolf was only Wave, and not someone trying to tear off his fur. "Oh, uh, hi," Nautilus stammered. "What are you... what brings you here?"

Wave turned around and bowed at Nautilus, making him feel squirmy inside his own fur. "Good morning, Prince Nautilus," Wave greeted. "King Delta has ordered me to fetch you for breakfast."

"Oh," Nautilus sighed. "Okay. I was hoping to see my friends this morning, but I guess they can wait." He fidgeted with the bracelet Aurora and Ember gave him, feeling guilty. Were they wondering where he was? It felt like moons had passed since Nautilus last saw them.

Wave curiously peered at Nautilus' bracelet, eyeing the painting of Aurora and Ember. "Your friends," she mused. "Are they wolves from other packs?"

Nautilus moved his wrist away from Wave, feeling embarrassed. He'd forgotten that most wolves didn't like the other elementals. Perhaps it was best if Nautilus didn't wear his bracelet in public anymore. It might lead to awkward questions, or suspicious looks.

"Sorry," Wave said. "I didn't mean to sound hostile. The truth is, I've never hated the other packs like most

Water Wolves do. I fear the other elementals, sure, but that's just fear of the unknown." Wave tossed her trident from paw to paw. "Do you mind if I ask what the other elemental wolves are like?"

Nautilus relaxed his tensed shoulders. "I don't mind at all," he replied as they swam through the castle. "They're wolves like any other. I find that everyone in Elementa is so concerned about what makes us different, that we forget to look at what makes us similar."

Wave nodded thoughtfully. "I've never looked at it that way before," she confessed. "I guess that if more wolves started thinking like that, we wouldn't try fighting one another all the time." Wave gave Nautilus a sidelong glance. "You're living proof that different packs can get along. It must feel surreal, to be a symbol of unity like that."

Nautilus faltered for a moment, feeling stunned. *A symbol of unity?* he thought. *Does Wave really think that?* Nautilus' ears flattened. *Do I even think that? I've always seen my existence as a mistake. In a divided world like this, there's no room for a hybrid.*

Nautilus gave his head a quick shake and continued swimming, not wanting Wave to think that something was wrong. He didn't allow the thought to linger in his mind. It was too overwhelming to ponder. Nautilus already hated being treated as royalty—as someone special. To think of himself as some symbol of unity was almost unbearable.

Eventually, Nautilus and Wave reached a pair of golden, ruby-encrusted doors. "We've arrived at the dining chamber," Wave told Nautilus. She bowed respectfully at him, then turned around, prepared to swim off.

"Wait," Nautilus said, just before she left. "Um, would you mind sticking around for a bit? I'm embarrassed to admit this, but I'm worried about, uh, dangerous wolves." Nautilus fidgeted with the webs between his paws. "If you don't have time to stay, that's totally fine. I understand that you're a commander of the guards, so if you can't..."

Wave's amber eyes filled with amusement, causing Nautilus to trail off. "You're royalty now, remember?" she asked, while trying to keep a straight face. "You don't need to ask nicely. Just say the word to me or anyone in the empire, and we'll do whatever you ask."

Nautilus frowned. "But that doesn't seem fair," he mumbled. "Why should I boss everyone around? Just because I have a fancy royal title?"

Wave looked startled. "Yeah," she replied. "That's the whole point of nobility."

Nautilus felt a sinking feeling grow inside his chest. "It is?" he asked in a small voice. If being a king meant bossing wolves around, then Nautilus wanted no part of it. Perhaps it was best to leave royalty to someone like Benthos, who enjoyed acting like he was above everyone else.

Wave cleared her throat. "It's best if you don't keep your father waiting," she said, trying to change the subject. "I'll stand on watch outside. Trust me. No 'dangerous wolves' will be entering this room."

"Thanks," Nautilus said. He opened the door and swam into the dining chamber, closing the door behind him. Nautilus felt an instant jolt of horror. Wave didn't need to prevent danger from entering the room—an enemy was already inside.

"Hello, Brother," Benthos sneered. "My, I thought you'd never show up. It certainly took you long enough." Although Benthos sat on the far side of the long table, his glare was so powerful that Nautilus felt it scorch into his fur.

"Where's Father—I mean, King Delta?" Nautilus demanded. He desperately tried to keep his voice from shaking.

Benthos dismissively waved a paw at Nautilus. "He's inspecting some new school that was built," he replied impatiently. "Now, let's save ourselves some time by skipping right to the answers of your clueless inquiries. I lied to Wave by telling her that Father was waiting for you here. I wanted to speak with you alone. And no, I'm not planning on killing you. Not at the moment." Benthos smiled unpleasantly. "Have a seat, Brother."

Nautilus nervously glanced at the shut doors, wondering if he should call Wave for help. *I can't seem like a coward in front of Benthos,* he told himself. *He's like a dangerous predator. If I show weakness, he'll pounce. Be strong, Nautilus.* Forcing back his fear, Nautilus sat down on the seat opposite of Benthos. The long table stretched between them, putting a comfortable distance between the two wolves.

A plate of fancy food rested in front of Nautilus. Although he was starving, he didn't dare touch his meal. Benthos could have very well poisoned it. With a gulp, Nautilus pushed his plate away from him.

Benthos smirked. "I've summoned you to discuss a truce," he announced unexpectedly.

Nautilus suspiciously gazed at his adopted brother. He didn't speak, remembering Wave's statement about how Benthos liked to twist whatever a wolf said for his own advantage. *What are you up to?* Nautilus thought.

"The truth is, the two of us know much more about the other than we'd like to admit," Benthos continued stiffly. "You know about my personal plans for the empire, once I become king. I know about you being a disgraceful mistake of a wolf." Benthos grinned wickedly. "We both have our secrets. We both have identities that would preferably be kept secret. Why don't we help each other do just that?"

Nautilus' eyes narrowed. "You don't seem like the type of wolf that likes to help others," he retorted.

Benthos' ears flattened. "I'll make an exception," he growled in a low voice. "Just this once. What do you say, Brother? Help me, help you. It's a win for both of us, after all." Benthos clasped his front paws together, smiling with anything but happiness.

Nautilus was silent for a very long time, carefully considering Benthos' offer. Nothing about it really screamed 'sinister' to him. Benthos only seemed concerned about protecting his own fur, and just happened to need Nautilus' help to do that. "Fine," he said. "I'll keep your secrets to myself as long as you give me the same courtesy."

Benthos' yellow eyes shone ghoulishly in the morning sunlight. "Marvelous," he rumbled. Without warning, Benthos abruptly rose to his paws and swam toward the door.

"Where are you going?" Nautilus asked, feeling a bit worried to let Benthos out of his sight.

Benthos flashed Nautilus a hostile grin as he swam by. "Oh, I just have a bit of royal business that I must attend to," he answered. "Nothing incredibly exciting. The usual."

Nautilus instinctively rose out of his chair and blocked Benthos' way. "Hold on," he said. "I want to know something before you leave." Benthos looked less than impressed, but Nautilus continued speaking anyway. "Our truce. Does this mean that the two of us are at peace now?"

Benthos tossed back his head and laughed. "Goodness, no," he chuckled. "But let me assure you that our little rivalry won't last much longer." Without saying another word, Benthos purposefully knocked into Nautilus while swimming past him. Benthos threw the doors open and entered the corridor beyond. He growled threateningly at Wave as he slithered away into the enormous castle.

Wave watched Benthos go with wide eyes. She then whipped around to face Nautilus, who was rubbing his sore shoulder with a paw. "What in Elementa happened?" Wave demanded as she burst into the dining chamber. "Was Benthos in here the entire time? Where's the king?"

"Benthos lied to you so he could speak with me alone," Nautilus explained. "It's okay, though. He only wanted to make a truce with me. Everything's fine."

Wave clutched her trident harder. "Everything doesn't seem fine to me," she growled. "Benthos sees you as a threat. He could've attacked while you were alone with him in there." Wave pressed a paw to her forehead, looking stressed. "Your destruction could've been all my fault." Wave removed her paw. Determination glowed in her amber eyes. "Prince Nautilus, from now on, I'd like to accompany you everywhere as your personal guard."

Nautilus felt flustered. "Everywhere?" he squeaked. "That seems a bit extreme, don't you think?" Visions of Wave hovering near him while he tried to sleep filled his mind. Nautilus shuddered. He wasn't the type of wolf that enjoyed the company of others.

Wave shook her head. "With all due respect, Your Majesty, I think guarding you at all times is the least I can do," she replied. Wave lowered her voice and said, "Don't tell anyone I said this, but I really, really don't like Benthos. If he ends up being king, he'll make the Water Pack Empire his own personal playground. It'll be a total nightmare."

Nautilus twiddled with his tail fins. "I appreciate the offer, Wave," he said, "but I'm okay on my own. Benthos is just one wolf, after all. The rest of the empire doesn't even know that I'm royalty yet. Nobody will bother me."

Wave looked sheepish. "About that," she said awkwardly. "King Delta was *sort of* telling the entire castle that his long lost son has returned."

"What?!" Nautilus gasped.

"Yeah," Wave said. "It all happened this morning while you were asleep. He was so proud that his 'true heir' has returned. Everyone was shocked. Trust me, Your Highness, word travels fast in this empire. I'm sure the entire pack knows you're royalty now."

Nautilus felt dizzy. *Everyone knows,* he thought in despair. Nautilus' royalty had just become real. Scarily real. This wasn't a secret that only a few wolves knew anymore. Now, hundreds upon thousands of wolves were aware of who he really was. How was Nautilus supposed to live a normal life now?

"I need to go," Nautilus whimpered. "Just for the day. I need a break. It's too much."

Wave lifted herself taller and tightened her grip around the trident. "Lead the way," she told Nautilus.

"No, please stay," Nautilus told her, feeling stressed out to the max. "I need to be alone."

Wave looked crestfallen. "But—"

"That's an order," Nautilus choked out, hating to use his royalty for his own gain. "If my father asks about me, tell him that I won't be gone forever. I just need to think things over." Without giving Wave a chance to protest, he turned around and swam out of the dining chamber.

As Nautilus navigated through the castle, and swam out to the empire, he could feel the eyes of everyone on him. Nautilus appeared to have captured the attention of the whole pack. There wasn't a single wolf who wasn't watching him.

Whispers slithered into Nautilus' ears as he rushed to the edge of the empire. *Not this again,* he thought with rising anxiety. *It's just like last time. So much staring. So much whispering. Why does this have to happen twice?!* Nautilus' head felt light. Black stars danced in his vision. His anxiety continued to grow worse and worse as he overheard the kingdom's gossiping.

"I can't believe that freak is King Delta's son," one wolf murmured.

"Hopefully that weirdo won't end up being king," another hissed.

"He doesn't have my support."

"Imposter." "Liar." "Mistake." "Fool."

Nautilus swam faster and faster, wanting to flee the empire as quickly as possible. He was careful to avoid speeding chariots this time. Getting run over once was plenty.

After what felt like forever, Nautilus finally left the last of the empire towers behind. He let out a sigh of relief as he reached the open ocean. *I did it,* Nautilus thought. *I'm safe.* He lightly ran a claw over his bracelet, feeling comforted by its presence on his wrist. *Now it's time to return to my true family.*

Nautilus swam through the ocean in silence, wanting nothing more than to reach the shores of Emora Island. He was hungry, tired, and filled to the brim with worry. However, it was his worry that kept him going. Nautilus felt out of place in the sea, now more than ever. He wanted nothing more than to escape the watery depths, and to feel dry land beneath his paws.

Oh, great! Nautilus thought happily. *There's the coral reef. I'm not too much further from Emora Island.* He eagerly quickened his pace. Before long, Nautilus was able to see the beginnings of the island. He'd made it back safely.

Or so he thought.

Paws abruptly wrapped around Nautilus' face, covering his eyes. At the same time, fangs sunk into his shoulder, turning the water red. Nautilus let out a cry of anguish.

A wolf was trying to kill him.

CHAPTER 12

Although Nautilus couldn't see, he could tell that his attacker was dragging him further below the surface. Water rushed past Nautilus' fur. Bubbles exploded out of his mouth as he screamed. Nautilus kicked and thrashed helplessly, but he couldn't break free from the attacker's hold.

Pain rushed through Nautilus' entire body. His heart was beating so fast that he'd thought it would burst out of his chest. Fangs sunk deeper into Nautilus' fur, causing a fresh wave of agony to scourge him. *This is the end!* Nautilus thought in despair.

No! I can't give up! Not now! Adrenaline thundered through his veins. *For once in my life, I need to fight! I can't let this wolf win. Fight. Fight!* Nautilus abruptly twisted around and tried to bite the arm of the wolf. His fangs merely snapped on nothingness.

I can't see a thing! Nautilus thought fearfully. He tried shaking off the paws of the wolf, but the attacker held on even tighter than before in retaliation. *I need to try something else. Hurry, Nautilus! Think!* He could feel his energy draining by the second. Nautilus needed to move quickly if he was to survive.

An idea suddenly struck him. It was dangerous, but it was the only chance he had.

Nautilus transformed into a Fire Wolf. He immediately started to suffocate. His gills had vanished—his lungs now screamed for air. Nautilus' webs and fish-like tail were gone, too, making him useless underwater. However, there was one advantage his Fire Wolf form gave him. Scorching, dangerous paws.

Nautilus blindly swiped a paw in his attacker's direction. Just before the attacker fled, Nautilus' paw met with fur, and the wolf cried out in pain. Relief flooded through Nautilus as the wolf released him. The attacker whirled around and swam away as fast as possible. Nautilus managed to catch only a brief glimpse of the wolf before his attacker disappeared into the coral reef. Had that been Benthos? It was so hard to tell.

Nautilus began to feel dizzy. He was drowning, and he didn't have the strength to make another transformation. With desperate, floundering strokes, Nautilus struggled to the surface. His head eventually broke out of the water. Nautilus gasped and wheezed for breath, hurriedly filling his lungs with air.

Thank goodness, he thought, coughing when he accidentally sucked in a mouthful of saltwater. *I survived.*

Nautilus' ears were ringing so fiercely that it took him a few moments to realize that wolves were screaming. He turned around, blinked the briny water out of his eyes, then spotted Aurora and Ember on the beach nearby. Panic was spilled across their faces.

"I'm okay," Nautilus weakly told them. "I'm fine. I..." Nautilus suddenly fainted.

He woke up in the island's meadow to find Aurora and Ember hovering over him. Nautilus yelped. He flinched backward, then gasped as pain zipped through his body. Nautilus turned to look at his shoulder. It was wrapped up in palm leaves like one massive bandage. A pounding headache gripped him, causing Nautilus to groan.

"Oh, good," Ember huffed. "You're alive. I thought you were going to bite the dust for sure."

Aurora looked mortified. "Nautilus," she began in a trembling voice. "What happened? Ember and I were sun bathing on the beach, and the next thing we knew, the water started to turn red. We didn't know what was happening." Aurora nearly retched. "That's when we saw you. Were you attacked, or was it just an accident?"

Nautilus' paws shook. "Someone attacked me," he said in a small voice. Nautilus transformed back into a Water Wolf, feeling safer in his most familiar form.

Ember looked disgruntled. "Why?" he demanded. "You're kind of annoying, but not so bad that someone would attack you. Who do you think did this?"

Nautilus looked past Aurora and Ember then stared into the distance. "I think it was Benthos," he confessed shakily.

"Benthos?" Aurora asked. "You mean the wolf that hit you with a chariot?"

Nautilus' ears flattened. "That's the one," he confessed. "He's also... my brother." Nautilus told his friends the entire story of how he'd gotten arrested by Wave, taken into the castle to be interrogated by Benthos, and then finally how he reunited with his father, King Delta. By the time Nautilus finished speaking, Aurora and Ember looked stunned.

"You're a prince?" Aurora asked. Her green eyes were wider than a full moon.

He nodded solemnly. "Prince Nautilus of the Water Pack Empire, apparently." Nautilus shuddered. "Argh. That feels so weird to say."

Aurora shifted her wings, looking bewildered. "It feels even weirder to hear," she murmured. "I guess this is a good thing. When—sorry, I mean—if you become king of the Water Pack, you'll unite the empire with the rest of Elementa. It'll make our mission that much easier."

"Unless Nautilus gets murdered beforehand," Ember muttered ominously.

"Excuse me?" Nautilus squealed.

Ember glared at him. "Don't act naïve," the Fire Wolf snarled. "Everyone knows that heirs to a throne have targets on their backs. Benthos' attack was only the beginning." Ember's orange eyes hardened. "When you're royalty, everyone wants you dead. Your siblings, your pack, even your so-called friends."

Nautilus suspiciously peered at Ember. *He sounds like he's talking from experience,* he thought. *But that can't be right. There's no way that Ember is royalty. He would have told us.* When Nautilus glanced at Aurora, he could tell that she was just as confused by Ember's statement. *Or, Ember would have at least told her.*

Aurora sat down weakly. "Maybe it's best to avoid the Water Pack altogether now," she thought out loud. "If what you say is true, Ember, then Nautilus isn't safe there anymore. Should we move on to the Earth Pack, to try to find Sandstorm?"

Ember rolled his eyes. "Sandstorm?" he spat. "I'd rather not deal with her any time soon. She's way too grouchy for my liking."

Nautilus had to hold back a laugh. *It takes a grouch to know a grouch,* he thought.

"And besides," Ember continued. "This is Nautilus' adventure. He's entitled to make his own decisions." Ember turned his sharp orange eyes back onto the wounded hybrid. "What do you want to do?"

Nautilus nervously fidgeted with his tail fins. "I... don't know," he confessed. "Part of me is terrified to return to the Water Pack. Another part of me wants to see my father and empire again. Is that wrong?"

Aurora was about to say something kind and heartfelt, but Ember spoke first. "This is your life to live, Nautilus," he said sharply. "But, this is also your life to sabotage. If I were you, I would flee the Water Pack forever, and never dare go near it again. It's the only way to stay safe." Memories clouded Ember's eyes. "The choice is entirely yours, though."

Nautilus gulped. His throat felt dry. With such a big decision like this, how could he possibly know what the right choice was? "I think I'll stay on the island until tomorrow," Nautilus told his friends. "My wounds should be healed by then, and it'll give me enough time to make a decision."

Ember responded with a disapproving snort. He walked away, then sat underneath the shade of a palm tree, not too far away from Aurora and Nautilus.

Aurora smiled kindly at Nautilus. "I think you're brave for wanting to think everything over," she told him quietly. "I can tell that your adventure has made you stronger. The old Nautilus would have wanted to flee to the far side of Elementa, without a second thought. It's a big accomplishment that you aren't letting your fear control you anymore."

Nautilus looked at the ground, watching as a ladybug crawled across a blade of grass. "I'm still scared, though," he sighed. "I'm still terrified of everything going wrong."

Aurora shrugged. "Everyone is afraid of something," she replied. "It's what we do with our fear that defines us."

"Anyway," Nautilus said, feeling awkward. "Do you think it's a good idea to go back? I've heard Ember's opinion, and now I want to hear yours, before making my choice."

Aurora gazed up at the sky, watching the clouds. "You were almost killed today, Nautilus," she said. "The worst part is that we don't even know by who. It could've very well been Benthos himself, or it might have been someone entirely different. We don't know who we're dealing with, and that terrifies me."

Aurora gave Ember a quick look. Once she was sure he wasn't listening, Aurora turned her head back to Nautilus. "I don't want to tell Ember this yet, but I think you should know right away," she whispered. "I was flying yesterday and I saw something... strange... on Elementa's coast, not too far from here."

Nautilus' eyes widened. "What was it?" he asked.

"Fire Wolves," Aurora explained. "Four of them. They were shouting at one another. Two of them even started fighting. I couldn't make out much of their words, but I overheard things that made my blood turn cold. They said 'rogues', 'traitor', 'capture', 'destroy', and I was even sure I heard someone shout Ember's name in the frenzy. It was hard to tell, though. I'm just thankful they were too busy arguing to notice me flying overhead.

Nautilus stiffened. "You don't think they had something to do with the attack earlier, do you?" he questioned.

"I don't think so," Aurora responded. "They can't swim underwater, and they shouldn't have anything against you, Nautilus. Royalty or not."

"So they aren't dangerous, then?" Nautilus asked with a growing sense of foreboding.

"I didn't say that," Aurora replied in a low voice. "They're definitely not friendly. Their camp was filled with cages. They had maps with claw marks slashed through the paper. I think they're hunting something... or someone." Aurora gave Ember a wary look.

"I can ask Ember if he knows the Fire Wolves," Nautilus suggested.

Aurora shook her head. "It's best if we don't say anything about this yet," she said. "I don't want to concern Ember. He's never had a good experience with Fire Wolves, and I don't want him doing something reckless if he learns that his former packmates are so close by."

"Okay," Nautilus said. "We'll keep the Fire Wolves to ourselves for now."

"What was that about Fire Wolves?" Ember abruptly asked. Nautilus jumped. Ember had materialized right beside the two wolves without them realizing. Apparently, Ember was much stealthier than Aurora and Nautilus had realized.

Aurora looked at Ember and smiled. "Nautilus was just telling me about his mother," she lied. "Right, Nautilus?" She gave him a meaningful look.

Nautilus squirmed under Ember's intense gaze. "Uh, yeah," he squeaked. "Father, I mean, King Delta said that her name is Ash."

"Ash?" Ember echoed. He paused for a long moment. Ember then blinked quickly a few times, snapping back to reality. "Uh, what happened to your mother, Nautilus? After... you..."

"Got separated from her?" Nautilus said for him. "I don't know. Not even my father knows what happened. At least, I don't think that he does." Nautilus frowned. "Maybe I can ask him more about her if I go back to the empire."

Ember nodded, a quick jerk of his head. "Do that," he said. Ember then turned around and walked away without saying another word. He was swallowed up by the jungle foliage, disappearing from sight.

"That was weird," Nautilus mumbled.

"He always gets weird when you mention Fire Wolves," Aurora explained. "See what I mean now? Ember will probably freak out if he learns about those four on the coast. Although I hate hiding things from him, we have to keep this a secret for now. There's no point burdening Ember until we learn more."

Nautilus nodded. As he did so, a yawn escaped from his snout. "Will you keep watching the Fire Wolves, then?" Nautilus asked sleepily.

"As long as you agree to get some rest now," Aurora responded. "Think carefully about your decision, Nautilus. I won't tell you what to do, but I ask that you please be cautious. You're one of my best friends, and I don't want anything bad happening to you."

Nautilus met her eyes. "I promise that I'll make the best decision I can," he answered.

"That's all I ask," Aurora responded. She unfolded her wings and leapt into the dusk sky. The golden light of the setting sun shone on her white pelt, turning her fur and feathers yellow. Aurora caught a current of wind and glided out of sight.

Nautilus was alone in the camp now. He heaved himself to his paws and limped toward his usual sleeping spot in the tall grass. Nautilus winced as he curled up to sleep. *This morning I woke up in a luxurious castle,* he thought. *Now I'm going to sleep with a torn-up shoulder. Someone tried to end my life today... and yet I survived.*

I managed to take care of myself. For once, I didn't need to rely on someone else to protect me. Nautilus' paws curled into tight fists. Determination glowed in his light green eyes. *Maybe I'm stronger than I think. If I was really so weak and pathetic, I wouldn't have been able to survive the attack on my own.*

Benthos thought he could get rid of me easily. He was wrong—I proved him wrong. And I'll prove him wrong, time after time if I have to.

I'm not a coward. Not anymore. I won't let my fear control me. I have the right to live in the empire... and I have a right to the throne. Benthos can try to scare me all he wants, but I won't let him win.

I'm Prince Nautilus of the Water Pack Empire, and I refuse to give up.

CHAPTER 13

Nautilus was wide awake, even before sunrise. He'd been unable to sleep for most of the night, and for the first time in forever, it wasn't because of fear. Nautilus was determined. He was ready to swim right back to the empire to show Benthos who's boss. There was no way Nautilus was going to let his kelp-brained brother think that he'd won.

This is only the beginning of our royal rivalry, Nautilus thought, *and I'm ready for whatever Benthos throws at me. I'm stronger than he thinks.*

Nautilus rose to his paws, rustling the tall grass around him. Pain gripped his shoulder, but the wound was recovering quickly. Nautilus silently crept away from his sleeping spot and strode across the meadow.

Stars glimmered in the violet sky, and the last of the moon's light fell over the island, illuminating the foliage. Nautilus gave his friends' treehouse a quick glance as he passed by it. There was no noise or movement coming from inside. His friends were still asleep. *I'll see you guys soon,* Nautilus thought. *At least, I sure hope I will.*

Nautilus' bravery began to waver as he stepped onto the beach. The sun was just beginning to rise in the horizon, turning the churning ocean gold.

Nautilus' pawsteps faltered and he halted near the water, just out of its reach. Memories of the attack swirled through his mind. Nautilus remembered the agony he'd felt when the wolf had sunk its fangs into his pelt. He remembered how he was dragged further below the surface. He remembered thinking that his life was about to be stolen from him.

Nautilus' fur spiked out in fear. He began to rethink entering the sea.

Remember what Aurora told me, he thought with a nervous breath. *It's what I do with my fear that defines me. I need to control my emotions, and not let them control me. I'm letting Benthos win if I give up.* Nautilus forced himself to walk into the ocean. Cool, salty water splashed his fur, rising steadily as he made his way further in. Once it was up to his neck, Nautilus plunged his head underwater.

It took a few moments for his eyes to adjust to the dim lighting. Odd shadows were cast across the ocean floor, while the coral and kelp had a yellow glow from the sunrise. Tiny fish zipped around Nautilus' face as he paddled forward. He held his breath. Would someone be waiting for him; to finish what the attacker had started?

All was silent as Nautilus cautiously glided through the water. After a few minutes of swimming, he allowed himself to relax. If a wolf was planning to ambush him this morning, it would have happened well before now. Perhaps Benthos had given up on destroying Nautilus, if he really was the wolf behind the attack.

I wonder what those Fire Wolves are up to this morning, Nautilus mused. *Would it be a bad idea to try finding them? I'd be safe in the water, and I won't dare go anywhere near them.* He paused for a moment. *No, I should leave the spying to Aurora, like we agreed. I need to get back to the empire and tell my father what happened. He needs to know that a wolf is set on ending my life.* Nautilus shuddered. *How will King Delta react when he hears that Benthos is probably the one responsible?*

The empire eventually emerged in the distance, vast and shimmering. Nautilus wasn't sure if he felt glad to see it, or terrified. The Water Pack offered protection and a place where Nautilus could call home. However, it also promised danger for a new, inexperienced prince. He desperately hoped that returning wasn't a mistake.

As Nautilus swam through the empire and to the castle, he noticed that wolves were no longer glaring at him. Now, they avoided acknowledging him altogether. Some wolves even went out of their way to flee from the new prince the moment they saw him coming. *Nobody wants to get on the wrong side of royalty,* Nautilus thought with a sinking feeling inside his chest. *Now that they know who and what I am, they're afraid of me. They probably think that I'm above them, too. But I'm not. I'm a wolf like any other.*

They don't see it that way, though, Nautilus realized. *Everyone must look at me and see a wolf just like Benthos. Greedy, selfish, arrogant, and condescending.* Nautilus clenched his jaw. *I don't blame them for thinking that. Having a prince like Benthos is all they've ever known. But I promise that if I ever take the throne, I'll be completely opposite from Benthos.* Nautilus was surprised by the fierce protectiveness he felt for his empire. Some instinct was kicking up inside of him—one that wanted to defend his pack while also challenging its enemies.

Nautilus was quickly overwhelmed by his powerful, unexpected emotions. He pushed them aside to clear his head. *Right now, I need to focus on one thing: exposing Benthos to my father. I'm certain that my brother is the one responsible for yesterday's attack. I won't let him get away with it. Nobody that wicked should be anywhere near the throne.*

Eventually, Nautilus reached the castle. His heartbeat quickened as he entered inside.

It was absolute chaos. Guards were rushing back and forth, while shouts filled the golden palace. What in Elementa was going on?! Nautilus hesitated by the entrance. In less than half of a second, a guard spotted him. "I found him!" the guard cried. "I found Prince Nautilus!"

Nautilus yelped as an armada of guards swarmed around him. Questions were thrown at Nautilus left, right, and centre. The noise was so much that his ears began to ring. *For the moon's sake!* Nautilus thought. *What is wrong with everyone?*

"Give him space!" a voice suddenly screamed, managing to rise above the chaos. "I said, give the prince space!" At her command, the guards dispersed around Nautilus. Commander Wave prowled forward with a scowl on her face.

"Wave!" Nautilus cried with relief. "What is going on? Why is everyone freaking out?"

Wave flattened her ears. Her amber-eyed gaze was as sharp as daggers. "Come with me, Your Highness," Wave told Nautilus. "*Now.*" Without giving him a chance to protest, Wave turned around to lead Nautilus through the castle.

Nautilus warily eyed the swarm of guards before swimming after Wave. He felt their gazes burn into his dark blue pelt the entire time. Thankfully, Wave and Nautilus turned a corner, leaving the others behind. The two wolves were silent for a painfully long moment.

"You look mad," Nautilus eventually whispered.

Wave came to a screeching halt. She whipped around and glared at Nautilus, spilling over with rage. "If you weren't a prince," Wave snarled, "I would tear the fur off your flesh. How could you do this to me?!"

Nautilus felt absolutely bewildered. "Do what to you?" he asked in a small voice.

Wave looked like she was about to explode with anger. "Oh, I don't know," she sarcastically hissed. "How about vanishing from the entire kingdom for a whole day? On my watch, no less!"

Nautilus shrunk under her furious glare. "But I told you I was going," he mumbled.

"In the vaguest way possible!" Wave growled. "Going where? Outside the castle? Outside the district? Outside the entire empire? Outside the ocean itself?! You left before I could even ask where you were heading!" Wave bared her fangs.

Nautilus fiddled with his tail fins. "Um," he stammered. "I don't mean to upset you, but does it really matter?"

Wave smacked a paw against her forehead. "Not for you, maybe," she retorted. "But for your empire, it absolutely does! King Delta was outraged and terrified when *I* had to tell him you disappeared. He sent out an entire search party, and nobody could find you. Some wolves feared that you were dead or hurt. The whole ocean was filled with unrest."

"Oh," Nautilus whispered.

"Oh?" Wave echoed in disbelief. "That's it? That's all you have to say for yourself?" Wave had to use every measure of self-control to avoid clawing Nautilus when he nodded. "Don't you understand how important you are to the empire? Without you, Benthos is going to become king, and he'll make the ocean a living nightmare. Nobody will be safe in his claws. I'll probably be the first wolf he annihilates if he becomes leader."

Nautilus' eyes widened with despair. Wave's description of the future sent panic bolting through his veins.

"Nautilus, you need to be more careful," Wave continued urgently. "The empire needs you more than anything else. We're doomed if Benthos becomes king—and you're the only one who can stand in his way. So don't you dare run off again!"

Nautilus was trembling from ears to tail. "I... I won't," he responded. "Not again. Not like that. I hadn't realized that I was so important to the Water Pack until now." Nautilus had only wanted to stand up to Benthos to prove himself. He hadn't thought about how opposing Benthos meant protecting not just his pride, but also the lives of so many innocent wolves.

Nautilus' head began to spin.

Wave impatiently lashed her pale blue tail. "Let's get moving, all right?" she snapped, pulling Nautilus out of his thoughts. "King Delta is waiting for the both of us."

"I'll make sure you don't get in trouble," Nautilus reassured her. "It isn't your fault that I left the empire."

Wave's eyes widened slightly. However, she said nothing as she swam forward, while looking straight ahead. Nautilus followed Wave silently. Would his own father punish him for causing the empire such a scare? Was that something parents normally do? Nautilus had absolutely no idea.

Nautilus gulped when they reached the throne room. Wave gave him one last unhappy look before throwing the doors wide open. Together, the two wolves swam inside.

King Delta sat on his golden throne, his fish-like tail messily hanging over the edge. His light blue fur was unkempt and in total disarray. His eyes were unfocused, revealing his lack of sleep last night. The king's paws shook slightly from exhaustion.

Prince Benthos hovered beside his adoptive father, reporting to him on something in a snooty voice. Nautilus was too far away to make out the words, but he had a funny feeling that the report was about him.

Benthos was the first to notice Nautilus' and Wave's arrival. He stopped speaking and gave them a cold glare. "Ah, look who finally decided to show up," Benthos sneered. "My dear brother and my most favourite guard. A pleasure indeed."

King Delta's eyes came back into focus. He glided off the throne and swam toward Nautilus, managing to look relieved, angry, and nervous all at once. "Nautilus," he whispered. "I'm... I'm... I'm furious with you! How dare you scare me like that?!" King Delta suddenly noticed the bite mark on Nautilus' shoulder. He released a gasp of terror. Anger then filled his eyes, so intense that Nautilus felt scared of his own father.

"WHO DID THIS TO YOU?!" King Delta roared.

Nautilus forced himself to look away from the king, turning his attention onto Benthos. He had a smug, nonchalant expression on his face. Nautilus peered at him carefully, wanting to see if there were any scorch marks on his steel-blue fur. However, Nautilus found nothing. *Benthos wasn't my attacker,* he realized. *If he was, he would have been burned when my paws touched him.* Nautilus' head reeled. *If Benthos wasn't the wolf who attacked me... who was?*

"Answer me!" King Delta demanded impatiently. "I need to know who did this. Whoever threatened my son will be punished severely!" He protectively swam closer to Nautilus, looking ready to fight an entire pack of wolves to defend his son.

Benthos smirked. "This is certainly touching," he chuckled. "But I'm afraid I need to be going now. The kingdom must be alerted that their *beloved* prince has returned." Benthos drifted toward the door, leaving before King Delta or Nautilus could respond. Wave watched Benthos go with a cold expression on her face. He turned a corner and vanished from sight.

Nautilus met King Delta's concerned gaze. "I didn't see who attacked me," he confessed shakily. "But... I think I know who was responsible."

King Delta adjusted his crooked crown, looking ready for battle. "Who?" he demanded. "Tell me and I'll feed them to the sharks."

Nautilus paused for a long moment, aware of the trouble he was about to cause. There would be no going back after this. "Benthos," Nautilus said quietly. "I think that Benthos is the wolf to blame."

King Delta's eyes narrowed. "Benthos?" he asked. "Benthos is your brother and my son. He would never harm anyone."

Wave swam forward. "I disagree, Your Highness," she said.

"Silence!" King Delta shouted at her. "I'll be dealing with you later." There was an ominous threat in his voice.

"Wave is innocent," Nautilus hurriedly interjected. "She isn't to blame for anything, Father. I snuck away.

I didn't tell her where I was going. I ordered her to stay in the castle, and to not follow me. Wave did everything right. Please, do not take your anger out on her. Wave doesn't deserve it."

King Delta didn't look happy. "Very well," he responded in a flat voice. "If that's what you wish, Nautilus." King Delta lifted himself taller. "What makes you think that Benthos is guilty of such a terrible crime? What proof do you have?"

Nautilus' heartbeat quickened. "He threatened me," he stammered. "Yesterday morning, while you were out inspecting the new school. Benthos was acting really suspicious. He told me that he had 'royal business to take care of', and afterward I was attacked. Benthos is definitely the wolf behind everything!"

King Delta looked disappointed in his son. "That isn't proof," he responded through gritted teeth. "That's an assumption, and a dangerous one at that." Without warning, King Delta broke off into a terrible coughing fit. It rattled his entire body.

"Father!" Nautilus cried. He swam closer, unsure of how to help. Nautilus had never realized how thin and frail King Delta looked. It made his heart twist into nervous knots.

"I'm fine," King Delta rasped, waving Nautilus away with a paw. "Stress makes it worse, and you're giving me quite a headache." King Delta grinned teasingly at Nautilus. "Look, I understand that you're scared. Being royalty isn't easy. Trust me, I know that better than anyone. In my first few days as king, I refused to even eat, because I was afraid of someone poisoning my food. It's normal to think that every wolf is out to get you. But, before long, you realize that you're panicking over nothing."

Nautilus' ears flattened. "But—"

"No buts," King Delta interrupted. "If you fled the empire yesterday because you were scared of Benthos, then I can assure you, you were overreacting. Benthos is a good wolf. Sure, he's a bit headstrong, but he's not murderous. I've known him for many years, and I'm certain that he would never hurt his own brother."

Nautilus' entire face filled with disbelief. He was tempted to protest, but knew better than to argue with a king. Nautilus' father had made up his mind, and there was no changing it now.

"If you're still worried about attacking wolves, I have a solution for that," King Delta said calmly. "From now on, I'll have a fleet of guards watching you, wherever you go. Wave! Please fetch some of the strongest members of your team."

"Wait!" Nautilus shouted, just before Wave swam off. "Father, don't you think that's a bit extreme? I mean, *everywhere* I go?" How was Nautilus supposed to visit Emora Island now? Not every wolf in the Water

Pack was accepting of the other elementals yet. Nautilus would be leading battle-ready guards straight to his friends.

King Delta looked less than impressed. "I'm not the one panicking over nothing, now am I?" he retorted. "Besides, it doesn't hurt to have some extra protection, does it? This is for your own good, Nautilus." He smiled awkwardly at his son. "I'm sorry if I'm coming off as bossy. But it's what a good parent should do sometimes, right?"

Nautilus smiled back, trying to hide his frustration. "I have no idea," he said honestly. "But if you insist on extra protection, can Wave be my only bodyguard?"

King Delta gave her a curious peer, looking like he was trying to decide whether he still trusted her or not. "I suppose," he responded stiffly. "If that's what you think is best, Nautilus."

Wave swam closer to Nautilus, then hovered a respectful distance away from the royals. "I won't let you down," she told Nautilus. Wave then looked at King Delta. "I promise that I won't disappoint you again, Your Highness."

King Delta gave her a nod. He then clasped his front paws together. "Wave, why don't you give Nautilus a tour of the empire?" he asked. "I've come to realize that my son hasn't had a proper introduction to our home yet. Although a grand celebration is in order, I gave my word not to push any royalty stuff on him." Despite the wink King Delta gave, the worry in his eyes was plain to see.

"You sound like you want me gone," Nautilus murmured cautiously. "Is everything okay, Father?"

King Delta looked guilty. "Everything is fine," he responded. "It's not that I want you gone, Nautilus. The opposite, in fact. It's just that I'm going to be doing some investigation around the castle. I know I should be leaving this to you and your guards, Wave, but I want to personally confirm Benthos' innocence and uncover the truth myself."

King Delta fiddled with his tail fins. "I don't want you to see me when I'm angry, Son. I've been told that I can come off as quite intimidating when I'm in a bad mood. You only saw a small portion of my grouchy side." King Delta smiled shyly.

Nautilus nodded vigorously. "I'll take your word for it," he replied. Nautilus turned to Wave. "Do you know any good places to eat? I'm starving."

Wave grinned. "I know a place," she responded.

Nautilus and Wave left the castle and swam into the underwater metropolis. Little did they realize that they were being watched. Wolves crept through the shadows, following Nautilus wherever he went.

The prince was being stalked.

CHAPTER 14

Nautilus was relieved when Wave led him away from the bustling empire. Throughout the tour, Water Wolves had avoided Nautilus like he had some type of plague. It had been bad enough to have wolves glare and mock him, but it was even worse when they treated him like he didn't even exist.

It made Nautilus feel squirmy, like his pelt was on too tight. He'd rather be treated badly, instead of being treated like he wasn't there at all.

Before long, the endless commotion of the empire faded away with distance, leaving the two wolves in peaceful silence. Tall strands of kelp swayed serenely in the cool current, while neat rows of coral lined the seashell-encrusted pathway. "Where are we headed?" Nautilus asked Wave. At the same time, his stomach growled. "Uh, is the restaurant you were talking about earlier over here?"

Wave shook her head. "There's one more thing I'd like to show you before we end the tour," she replied. "I think this is important for you to see." Without elaborating any further, Wave swam ahead, scanning the area for any possible danger.

Nautilus didn't say it, but he thought that nothing was more important than food right now. He'd literally die of hunger if he didn't get something decent to eat soon. He was absolutely starving. *I've waited this long to eat, so I guess I can wait a little bit more,* Nautilus thought miserably. He let out a pitiful sigh and kept on swimming.

Something shiny up ahead suddenly caught Nautilus' eye. Further along the path were dozens of statues, all shimmering majestically in the sunlight. They each depicted a Water Wolf in a dynamic pose. Some wolves looked fierce, like they were in the middle of a battle. Other wolves looked regal and calm, while others appeared to be giving a wise speech.

"Who's all this?" Nautilus asked, slowing down so he could study each statue carefully. He realized that every Water Wolf had a crown on top of his or her head. "Are these my ancestors?"

Wave nodded. "Welcome to the Royal Memorial," she said. "This is where every noble wolf in our history is documented and remembered. The statues at the start of the path are of the most ancient wolves, while the ones at the end are of the most modern." Wave tossed her trident from paw to paw. "There will be a statue of you in here one day, Nautilus."

Nautilus' eyes widened. He felt startled to see so many wolves, and to know that he was related to each of them. Nautilus had grown up alone, with nobody to turn to. It had never come to mind that he had such a long and complicated bloodline. And these wolves were only from his father's side! How many more Fire Wolves were part of Nautilus' family tree? Probably too many to count.

Nautilus swam through the Royal Memorial in awe. He took his time, wanting to absorb as much as he could about his ancestors. It had never occurred to Nautilus that he had the blood of fierce warriors, wise scholars, and diplomatic negotiators in his veins.

I carry a part of each of these wolves within me, Nautilus realized. *If they could see me now, would they be proud of me? I'm working hard every day to be strong like them. I've made so much progress since beginning my journey. Have I brought honour to my kin?* Nautilus hoped so.

Eventually, he reached the end of the path, coming face-to-face with a statue of King Delta. Close beside Nautilus' father was a statue of Benthos, who looked just as smug here as he did in the flesh. "I'll give credit where credit is due," Nautilus said jokingly. "The sculptors captured Benthos perfectly."

Wave chortled, causing a torrent of bubbles to tumble out of her gills. "Did you enjoy the Royal Memorial?" she asked, once she recovered from her laughing fit.

"I loved every moment of it," Nautilus responded truthfully. "Thanks for showing it to me. I'm glad I got to see it." He hesitated, fiddling with his tail fins. "Wave? I was just wondering if any of these wolves were hybrids?"

Wave instantly shook her head, not even needing a moment to think about it. "No," she said decidedly. "You're the only royal hybrid in the Water Pack's history."

"Oh," Nautilus whispered, feeling that familiar sense of isolation creep back into his heart.

Wave looked awkward, unsure of how to respond. An uncomfortable silence fell over the two wolves for a painfully long moment.

"Do you think the Water Pack will ever accept me, if they learn about my Fire Wolf side?" Nautilus asked suddenly. Wave managed to look more uncomfortable than before. "You can tell me the truth, Wave. I want to know what you really think."

"Well," Wave said slowly. "The truth is, I'm not sure how the empire will react. Hybrids are extremely rare. You may even be the first one in centuries, Nautilus. The empire might be *slightly* daunted to learn that their heir is half Fire Wolf."

Nautilus drooped pathetically.

"But there's nothing wrong with being a hybrid!" Wave said quickly, not wanting Nautilus to be upset. "You might have to work extra hard to earn the empire's approval, but that's all. I'm sure the Water

Wolves will love you, once they get to know you. They just need a chance to see why you're the best choice for king. And trust me, if their only other option is Benthos, you won't have a hard time convincing them." Wave winked.

Nautilus perked up, feeling more confident than before. "You're right," he said. "Once everyone sees that I care about them, they'll probably support me, hybrid or not. Thanks, Wave." Nautilus smiled giddily, feeling excited to think that he may have supporters one day.

If I become king, I'll make sure that I'm the best leader possible, he thought. *I refuse to be anything like Benthos. There's no way that I'll let my empire be bullied by someone like him. My brother will have to go through me if he wants to harm the Water Wolves... even if that means taking the crown for myself.*

Nautilus still wasn't sure if he felt comfortable being a leader yet, but if becoming king meant stopping Benthos, then he supposed he could get used to it.

Nautilus was about to say something heroic and brave, but before he could, his stomach growled fiercely.

"Ready for some lunch, Your Majesty?" Wave asked teasingly.

Nautilus nodded vigorously. "Absolutely," he replied. Wave swam away, patrolling the path ahead to ensure the prince's safety. Nautilus hesitated for a brief moment, staring up at the statue of Benthos from underneath its shadow.

I'm ready for you, Brother, Nautilus thought. *You can send wolf after wolf to scare me, harm me, or even kill me. But it won't work. I'm stronger now. Stronger than ever before. My fear no longer controls me, and I'm determined to protect the empire from you. Give me everything you got, Benthos. I'm ready for the challenge.*

Nautilus swam away, leaving Benthos' statue behind. He could feel its cold, stone gaze watching his every move as he exited the Royal Memorial.

***

Nautilus' mouth watered as Wave led him into the Food Market at the empire's edge. The space was bustling and rowdy as hundreds of wolves swam from place to place. Nautilus couldn't believe how many booths were set up. He spotted stands that sold fresh seaweed wraps, clams by the dozen, lobster tails, and every other delicacy Nautilus could imagine.

"Order up!" a chef shouted.

"This Krill Surprise is the best," a wolf exclaimed.

"Yummy!" a pup declared. "I love kelp rolls!"

Nautilus felt overwhelmed and fascinated at the same time. "Where should we eat?" he asked Wave, struggling to make himself heard over the chaos.

"Wherever you want," Wave said, a slight edge to her voice. Her webbed paws tightly gripped her trident, while her amber eyes hurriedly scanned the area. Poor Wave. It must be difficult to guard a prince when he was surrounded by hundreds of unidentified wolves. There was so much danger here—so much that could go wrong.

"Whatever you do," Wave sternly told Nautilus, "do not leave my side."

"Ooo, look at that!" Nautilus said. He immediately left her side, swimming away. Before Wave could even react, Nautilus was swallowed up by the storm of wolves, vanishing from her sight. Nautilus was so transfixed that he didn't even notice his separation from Wave.

There was a large crowd of Water Wolves up ahead, distracting Nautilus from his hunger. He swam to them eagerly, wondering what they were watching. A crab race? A musician? When there was a crowd, there was normally something fun happening.

When wolves spotted Nautilus' approach, they immediately darted out of his way, forming a rift in the crowd. "Here comes Number Two," someone muttered. "Isn't one royal pain enough?"

Nautilus faltered. Royal pain? Number Two? Oh no. That could only mean—

"You messed up my order!" came Benthos' growl. He loomed over the two chefs that trembled inside their booth. "I wanted extra starfish crumbles, not seaweed sprinkles. Get it right!" Benthos tossed his meal right at the faces of the chefs.

"Yes, Your Highness," one of the chefs whimpered. She nervously adjusted her apron.

"We'll fix this right away," said the other chef. He looked terrified of the enraged prince.

Benthos stared at the two chefs coldly, watching as they scrambled to recreate his order. "Hurry up!" Benthos spat. "I'll be sending you straight to the Outer Islands if you waste any more of my time!"

Nautilus' eyes lit up with rage. "Hey!" he shouted. Benthos whipped around with a snarl, looking livid. "Leave those wolves alone!" Without thinking, Nautilus swam right to Benthos, feeling his heart pound with anger.

Benthos pulled back his lips to reveal his serrated fangs. "What are you going to do about it?" he challenged. "Lecture me to death?"

Nautilus instinctively growled back at Benthos, feeling ready to spring at his brother.

The crowd looked terrified to see two princes at once—especially when those two princes were at each other's throats. This was certainly going to end badly.

The Food Market had grown significantly quieter in the last few moments, while the crowd steadily became larger and larger. Everyone wanted to see what would happen next. Would the two heirs end up fighting? Would their royal rivalry be settled here and now, once and for all?

"Why don't you swim right back to whatever hole you crawled out of?" Benthos hissed at Nautilus. "Get out of my ocean before I make you. I'll tear you to shreds!"

Nautilus met Benthos' seething glare, trying not to flinch. Then, Nautilus spotted something from the corner of his eye. There was something small swimming away from the booth, heading toward the open ocean beyond. *Huh?* Nautilus thought. *What is that?* He broke his gaze away from Benthos to get a better look.

It was a tiny, newborn pup, one that looked just like the two chefs. With everyone distracted, the chefs' pup had managed to swim away unnoticed.

Before Nautilus could warn the pup's parents, Benthos suddenly slashed his claws across Nautilus' cheek. "Look at me, you fool!" Benthos shrieked. "It's time you and I settle this for good. I challenge you to a Battle of Power—a fight to the death!"

The crowd gasped.

Nautilus was so concerned about the pup that Benthos' challenge barely registered. The tiny bundle of fur was wandering further and further into the untamed ocean. "Not right now," Nautilus mumbled distractedly, turning around to get a better look at the pup. Nautilus pressed a paw against his wounded cheek, trying to stop the flow of blood.

"Excuse me?!" Benthos screamed. "Not right now? I'll murder you on the spot, you writhing worm!"

Nautilus gasped. In the distance, a colossal shark suddenly emerged from the murky water—then headed straight toward the pup.

"NO!" Nautilus cried. He zoomed past Benthos, accidentally sending him spinning through the water.

Nautilus exploded toward the pup at breakneck speed. The shark opened its gaping mouth, ready to devour the pup in one merciless bite. Just before it could strike, Nautilus scooped the pup in his paws, then thundered out of the shark's path.

Nautilus hadn't been fast enough.

The shark's jagged teeth sliced through Nautilus' fur, just before he could completely get out of the way. Nautilus hit the ocean floor with a thud. Agony flashed through him. Three long cuts snaked down his side, burning painfully in the salt water.

Thankfully, the pup was completely unharmed. But that didn't mean the two wolves were safe yet.

The shark rounded on them, ready to deliver another blow. Nautilus curled his body around the pup, trying to shield it. He slammed his eyes shut, waiting for the end to arrive... but it never did. Nautilus jumped at the sound of growling and shouting. He opened his eyes to find Wave and a fleet of guards driving the shark back.

"Get out of here!" Wave ordered Nautilus. "We'll handle this from—" Her words were cut off as she dove, avoiding the swinging tail of the shark.

Nautilus didn't need to be told twice. He held the pup close to his chest as he swam away, moving as fast as his wounded body allowed. *OW!* Nautilus thought, clenching his teeth. *What is with me getting injured on this journey?! First, I got hit by a speeding chariot. Next, some wolf attacked me. Then, I got chomped by a shark!*

Nautilus was fading in and out of consciousness as he stumbled back to the Food Market. The only thing that kept him from fainting was the cheering of the Water Wolves. He blinked hazily.

It took Nautilus a few moments to realize that they were cheering for *him*.

Nautilus couldn't believe it. Was this a dream?

"Prince Nautilus! Prince Nautilus! Prince Nautilus!" The Water Wolves started to chant his name, over and over again.

Benthos was spilling over with rage. As Nautilus fumbled back into the empire, Benthos whirled around and swam away, disappearing into the shadows. Nobody appeared to care about his absence. Everyone's attention was on Nautilus. Even Wave and the guards, who had successfully driven away the shark, watched the young prince attentively as they swam back to the empire.

The two chefs suddenly darted to Nautilus' side. "Here," he said weakly, passing the tiny pup back to its parents. Nautilus' paws and arms trembled. "Don't worry. Your pup wasn't hurt."

The chefs scooped up their pup frantically, looking shaken. "How can we ever repay you?" one asked Nautilus in a trembling voice.

Nautilus was tempted to ask for a free meal, since he was *still starving*, but decided to keep his mouth shut.

"Everyone back up!" Wave suddenly demanded. "Give the prince some space! Move out of the way. Clear a path. Hurry!" She rushed to Nautilus' side, then nearly retched when she saw his wounds. "That looks really painful. Hang on, Nautilus. I'm taking you to the royal medics."

Wave heaved Nautilus onto her back, making him feel beyond embarrassed. However, he was too weak to protest. Wave carried Nautilus toward the castle, while the fleet of guards surrounded the injured prince on all sides.

"Wave?" Nautilus choked out.

"I'm here," she responded.

"This is really embarrassing," Nautilus said.

Wave let out a terse laugh. "I think the empire is loving it," she said. "A hero wounded in action, while saving a pup, no less? I'm not trying to make light of your situation, but this moment couldn't be any more perfect."

It felt like the world was spinning around Nautilus. "Perfect for what?" he groaned.

"Perfect for the rise of Prince Nautilus' popularity," Wave responded. "I believe the empire has a new favourite heir."

CHAPTER 15

Nautilus blankly stared at the infirmary's marble ceiling, feeling bored out of his mind. He fiddled with his bracelet, wishing that he could go see Aurora and Ember. "Can I leave now?" Nautilus asked one of the medics, who was sorting supplies beside him. "I'm feeling a lot better now."

Wave, who was sharpening her trident by the door, gave Nautilus a quizzical look. "You've only been in here for twenty minutes," she said, trying to keep a straight face.

Nautilus buried his head in his pillow, groaning. "It feels like it's been forever," he responded in a muffled voice.

"Apologies, Your Highness," said the medic, while adjusting her crooked glasses. "It's best if you stay here for a bit longer so we can make sure your wounds heal correctly. That was one nasty injury. You're lucky that shark didn't gobble you up alive." She laughed nervously, then hurriedly returned to her work.

Nautilus lifted his head to gaze out the window, wishing he could do anything but sit here.

Without warning, the door swung open, and King Delta exploded into the room. Wave nearly jumped out of her fur. She shuffled backward to avoid getting trampled by the king. "Nautilus!" he cried. "Will you be all right?"

King Delta suddenly had a terrible coughing fit. His body violently trembled, while the water around him filled with a haze of bubbles. King Delta had to clutch the side of Nautilus' bed to avoid collapsing.

Nautilus swam forward to help his father stand. "Are you okay?" he fearfully asked. "Your coughing is getting worse and worse."

King Delta waved Nautilus away with a paw. "I'm fine," he said in a choked voice. "I'm going to be okay." Nautilus could tell that his father was lying. For the first time, he realized how weak King Delta had become in the last few days. His ribs were visible beneath his light blue fur, and there were dark bags beneath his green eyes. King Delta's paws trembled without ceasing, and his ears drooped.

"Here, Your Majesty," the medic said, passing a woven pouch to the king. "The herbs inside will lessen your cough."

King Delta took the pouch graciously. "Thank you," he huffed. "But I haven't come for this." King Delta put the pouch aside, then moved closer to Nautilus. "Tell me what happened, Son. I heard something about pups and sharks." King Delta anxiously fidgeted with his tail.

Nautilus told his father the whole story. He didn't try to hide how cruel Benthos was to the chefs, and echoed the threats he had received from his brother, word by word.

"Benthos said what?!" King Delta roared, after Nautilus had finished speaking.

Nautilus winced. "He challenged me to a fight to the death," he mumbled. "He said he would murder me on the spot if I didn't accept his proposal." Nautilus pointed at the slash mark on his cheek. "Benthos did this to me, and he would've done worse if I hadn't swum away to save the pup."

King Delta placed a paw on his forehead, looking dizzy. "I overheard him talking about a Battle of Power to his advisors a few nights ago," he whispered. "But I didn't think he was serious. I thought Benthos would have gotten along with you by now, Nautilus." King Delta looked sick. "I didn't want to think that Benthos loathed you so much. I tried so hard to prove to myself that he would never hurt you. But I was foolish to ignore what was right in front of me."

King Delta's light blue fur bristled. "I couldn't find any evidence that Benthos *wasn't* the wolf behind your attack," he admitted. "I searched the entire castle and interrogated as many wolves as I could. Unfortunately, it's very possible that Benthos is the culprit. There's no proof to suggest otherwise."

Nautilus fidgeted with his bracelet, feeling like the walls were closing in on him. "Father?" he asked in an unsteady voice. "I was just wondering if you've seen Benthos lately?"

King Delta paused. "I haven't seen him since this morning," he said in a quiet voice. "Why do you ask?"

"Because he swam away right after the Water Wolves started cheering for me," Nautilus responded nervously. "He looked angry. Very angry. I'm worried that he's planning something terrible... something even worse than the original attack."

King Delta's eyes were as hard as diamonds. "Benthos wouldn't dare," he hissed. "Not while I'm here to protect you."

And how much longer will that be? Nautilus wondered sadly. *Once it's just Benthos and I, what measures will my brother take to ensure that the throne is his?* Nautilus was dreading to find out.

"Don't worry about a thing, Son," King Delta continued. "I'll keep a close watch on Benthos, and the moment I see him again, I'll talk him out of any vile plans he has. I promise that everything will be okay. Nothing bad is going to happen to my son."

There was a long moment of silence.

"Father?" Nautilus eventually asked. "Can I ask you something in private?"

King Delta looked startled. "Of course," he responded. Wave and the medics briskly left the room at the king's command. Nautilus felt relieved. This was the first time he's ever been alone with his father. It was nice to have King Delta's company without an audience. "What's on your mind, Nautilus?"

Tell him the truth, Nautilus told himself. *Don't hold back any longer. I'm ready. I've grown so much on my journey. It's time to take the next step in realizing my true potential. I'm not a coward anymore. I'm not terrified of failure like I used to be, and I'm not afraid of Benthos. The kingdom supports me now. I've made friends. I've found my place.*

It's time I embrace my destiny, and become the wolf I'm meant to be.

"I'd like to become king," Nautilus confessed. "I'm ready to be an official heir. I know I was hesitating a lot earlier, but I'm willing to take the crown whenever the time is right."

King Delta looked proud, shocked, and impressed all at once. "Are you sure this is what you want?" he asked.

"I'm sure," Nautilus responded. "It just feels right. I won't lie and say that I'm not freaking out about this decision, because I am. I absolutely am. But I just know in my heart that this is what I'm meant to do.

Destiny brought me to you and the castle for a reason. How can I deny my own fate, and let fear control me?"

King Delta took off his crown, then grinned at Nautilus. "Want to try it on?" he asked.

Nautilus' paws shook slightly when he took the crown. He held his breath as he placed it on his head.

"Well?" King Delta asked with a smile. "How does it feel?"

Nautilus released a long breath, feeling a whirlpool of emotions. "It feels... amazing," he confessed. "It fits perfectly, like it's always belonged on my head."

King Delta managed to smile even brighter than before. "It looks good on you," he mused. "Nautilus, you look like a true leader. I know that you're going to do great things for the Water Pack Empire."

Nautilus returned the crown to his father. "I'll do my best," he said. Nautilus' gaze travelled down to his bracelet. "Father, would it be okay if I go meet my friends? I want to tell them that I've decided to become king."

King Delta paused for a moment, looking unsure of how to respond. "Nautilus, you do realize that I'll need to teach you everything I know before you become king, right?" he said. "I don't mean to worry you, but I'm in my final days, so there isn't much time to prepare you for leadership."

"Oh," Nautilus whispered.

"I'm truly sorry, but I'm afraid your friends will have to wait," King Delta continued. "The most difficult part of being a leader is that sometimes, the path you walk must be travelled alone. Nautilus, as king, you must give up plenty for the sake of your citizens. Are you prepared to do that?"

Nautilus nodded. *If that's what it takes to keep Benthos from obtaining power, then I'm prepared to do anything,* he thought determinedly.

"I'm proud of you, Nautilus," King Delta said. "You're so much stronger than you think. I can tell that you'll be an excellent leader—perhaps the best leader the Water Pack has ever known."

Nautilus was flustered by his father's praise. "I'm not sure about that," he said with a nervous laugh. "But I promise that I'll do my very best."

King Delta nodded. "That's all I ask," he responded. "Now, let's get to work. It's time to begin your first lesson."

CHAPTER 16

Nautilus woke up to a light tap on his door. He had to hold back a groan. *Great,* he thought. *Another early morning lesson on how to properly hold a fork.* Outside his balcony, the ocean was dark, and the moon could still be seen from the surface. *Wow. Father chose to start today's lesson really early.*

Two weeks had passed since Nautilus officially decided to become king. His father had taught him so much during that time—diplomacy, strategy, negotiation, traditions, and everything in between. Nautilus was finally feeling ready to become king. He was scared, though, and quite overwhelmed. Nautilus missed his friends every day, and wished that he could visit Emora Island just once. But there was no time for things like socializing.

To make Nautilus' stress even worse, Benthos had completely vanished from the empire. Nobody had seen him since the day Nautilus had become the pack's favourite heir. King Delta had sent out search party after search party to find Benthos, but every attempt had been unsuccessful. It was like Benthos had left the ocean altogether...

Nautilus' door was knocked on again, more urgently this time. "I'm coming," he called sleepily.

Nautilus batted away the tentacles of the jellyfish, who, for some reason, still hadn't left his room yet. Nautilus had decided to keep the jellyfish as a pet, and named it Squishy. The jellyfish didn't budge when Nautilus pawed it, and merely shocked him with a small jolt.

Frustrated, Nautilus untangled himself from Squishy, then paddled off his bed. He placed Flippers the plush dolphin on his pillow, wiped the drool from his mouth, then groggily opened the door. His eyes widened. "Wave? What are you doing here? Is everything okay?"

Wave looked stricken with concern. "No," she gasped. "You need to come with me quickly. It's your father. King Delta wants to speak with you as soon as possible. He's... he's..." Wave couldn't bring herself to finish.

Nautilus felt despair crash down on him. "I'm coming," he choked out.

Together, the two wolves rushed through the moonlit castle, heading toward the king's room. Nautilus' head was reeling. He felt sick, and every breath he took was a struggle. The corridors felt infinitely longer than they had before, while the castle seemed much larger than normal. The swim to King Delta seemed to go on for a lifetime.

Eventually, Nautilus reached the closed doors. He felt weak, and on the verge of collapse. However, he needed to stay strong. That's what a true leader would do. "Secure the area," Nautilus ordered Wave, forcing his voice to sound steady. "See to it that nobody disturbs us."

Wave nodded. "Yes, Prince Nautilus," she responded.

Nautilus' paw trembled as he opened the doors. With a deep breath, he swam inside. Lanterns of glowing moss floated through the room, softly shining on the medics who were quiet and grim. When they saw Nautilus, they left the room in silence, closing the door on their way out.

"Father?" Nautilus gently asked. "I'm here."

King Delta was curled up on his bed. He didn't move for a very long moment, and for a heart wrenching second, Nautilus thought that he'd arrived too late. Then, King Delta lifted his head and gave Nautilus a weak smile. "Hey, Son."

Nautilus swam to his side. "Is there anything I can do for you?" he asked in a cracked voice.

King Delta shook his head. "You've already done so much for me," he whispered. "It's time that I do something for you." King Delta coughed. "You might want to sit down for this. What I'm about to tell you might be... overwhelming."

Nautilus nervously allowed himself to sink to the floor. He curled his tail around his body, trying to comfort himself.

King Delta coughed again. "I'm sorry for leaving this to the last moment," he rasped. "I didn't want to cause you unnecessary stress. Not until you were ready to hear the truth."

Nautilus tried to speak, but no words would come out. Instead, he weakly nodded. Nautilus hoped that the look in his eyes would speak for him. *I'm ready to hear whatever you have to say,* he thought. *Don't leave anything you want to tell me unsaid.*

"Nautilus, it's time I told you more about your mother," King Delta murmured. "I've been keeping secrets from you, only to protect you from the truth. I hope you can forgive me." He coughed. "Shortly after I became king, I sent spies to the Fire Pack Dominion. I wanted to find out what happened to you and Ash, after the three of us were separated. I discovered more than I had hoped to find."

Nautilus' eyes widened.

"After my parents sent guards to take you away from Ash, she moved back to the Fire Pack Dominion," King Delta continued in a weak voice. "She told no one about you or me, and lived a quiet life for many moons. My spies overheard Fire Wolves talking about how Ash wasn't the same as she used to be. She was heartbroken after losing us."

King Delta's ears flattened miserably. "Ash managed to find a fresh start at life, though," he explained. "She befriended a Fire Wolf named Inferno, and the two eventually became mates. Over time, Inferno rose through the ranks, and ended up becoming king of the Fire Pack. Ash became queen."

The world spun around Nautilus. He was so overwhelmed that he couldn't even formulate proper thoughts.

King Delta was silent for a moment, wanting to give Nautilus a chance to process everything he had told him. "King Inferno and Ash had pups together, moons later," King Delta explained after a few seconds. "Nautilus, you have five Fire Wolf half-siblings."

Nautilus couldn't speak. Couldn't move. Could barely even breathe. *I share blood with five Fire Wolves,* he thought numbly. "Who?" Nautilus choked out. He couldn't manage to force out another word.

King Delta shook his head. "I don't know," he responded. "My spies were discovered on Fire Pack land shortly after the pups were born. They all barely escaped with their lives. I didn't want to risk the safety of any more Water Wolves, so I didn't send anyone back to investigate further. I'm so sorry, Nautilus, but now you know as much as I do."

Nautilus clenched his teeth and hung his head. "It's for the best that I don't know who my siblings are," he said in an unsteady voice. "And it's best that they don't know me. Other than sharing Ash as a parent, the six of us have nothing in common. It's better if we're separated."

King Delta hesitated. "I think so, too," he said slowly. "There's been rumours floating around Elementa for a while now. Rumours about King Inferno. He wasn't always the cruel monster he is today. Apparently, King Inferno has become this way due to a broken heart. He lost Ash a few moons after their pups were born."

"My mother is dead?!" Nautilus cried.

King Delta looked startled. "No, no," he said in a reassuring voice. "Ash is still alive... probably. She vanished one day from the Fire Pack without telling anyone, and has never been seen since." King Delta weakly fiddled with his tail fins. "Nobody knows why Ash abandoned the Fire Pack, but they have their guesses, just like I have mine. Nautilus, I believe Ash left in search of you."

Nautilus' mouth fell open in shock. After so many years of being alone, he never would have guessed that his mother was somewhere out there, searching for him. It was almost too good to be true. "That's just speculation," Nautilus pointed out.

"Speculation is all we have," King Delta said softly. "Although I'll be leaving you soon, you can have peace of mind knowing that your mother may be somewhere out there. Nautilus, don't ever think that you're alone in this world. You've made friends. You've found your family. You have the support of the pack. Nobody is more loved than you, Son."

Nautilus gently placed his paw on his father's. "I'm glad that I was able to meet you," he said. He tried to speak again, but couldn't bring himself to utter another word, thanks to the lump in his throat.

King Delta smiled at his son, tears streaking down his face. He moved his paw away from Nautilus, then slowly took off his crown. "Here," King Delta said, passing the crown to his son. "I believe that this belongs to you."

Nautilus placed the crown on his head with bitter joy. His own tears began to flow. King Delta gently wiped them away with his paw. "Go, Son," he whispered. "Go and meet your empire. You belong among the living. Accept what is new and don't cling to the past. Your memories are there to strengthen you, not hinder you."

King Delta's breath was slow and shallow. "Go be the wolf you're meant to be," he said quietly. "Make me proud."

"I don't want to leave you," Nautilus whimpered, feeling his heart shatter. "I wish there was more time. But although we weren't together for very long, I can say with certainty that you're the best father I could have ever wished for."

King Delta, with the last of his strength, wrapped his arms around Nautilus and pulled him into a hug. "And I couldn't have asked for a better son," he whispered. "But now it's time for you to go."

Nautilus hesitated for a long moment before turning around. He forced himself to leave the room, to carry out his father's last wish. It was the most difficult thing he'd ever done in his life. Nautilus paddled away, tears blurring his vision. Wave watched him go sadly, looking like she wanted to fight to protect Nautilus. However, this was an enemy that Wave couldn't fight. The battle for inner peace was one only Nautilus could confront.

The sun was beginning to rise outside the castle's many windows, filling the ocean with pale light. It was the start of a new day, and of a new chapter for the Water Pack.

Nautilus swam purposefully through the castle, not allowing himself to give in to his grief. When the castle's helpers spotted the crown on top of Nautilus' head, they bowed respectfully at their new king. It still felt strange for Nautilus to be seen as someone powerful. He wasn't sure if he'd ever get used to it.

Eventually, Nautilus swam out to one of the castle's largest balconies. It was made of pure gold that shimmered in the morning sun. Nautilus slowly made his way to the railing, then leaned on it, grimacing. A cool current ruffled Nautilus' fur and whispered in his ears. He could see the entire empire from up here. From this height, his home looked so small—so fragile and helpless in this massive world.

The Water Pack needed someone to lead them. They needed a worthy wolf to guide them through whatever hardships life threw at them. Nautilus wasn't sure if he was that wolf, or if he ever would be. He had his father's legendary reputation to live up to.

My father—the previous king of the empire— believed in me, Nautilus thought. *The pack believes in me, too. So do my friends. Since the very beginning, wolves have supported me, cheering me on. The only one who never saw me as worthy was myself.* Nautilus' paws curled tighter around the railing. *I see now that I was always the one holding me back. But not anymore. I've realized my true potential. I'm not afraid of failure any longer, because it's failure that allows me to grow stronger.*

Whatever life throws at me, I'm ready. No more hesitation. No more living life in fear. No more doubts. It's time I embrace my destiny.

Nautilus howled. His call filled the silent empire, echoing through the streets and golden towers. Wolves immediately began to swim to the courtyard, just like King Delta had said they would. Nautilus had been taught well.

Before long, the courtyard was packed with wolves, who all looked anxious to see what the new king had to say. Nautilus had the attention of hundreds upon thousands of wolves. And yet, Nautilus wasn't nervous. He actually felt at peace, like this was what he was meant to do all along.

Their murmuring and hushed words filled the ocean. Nautilus could hear concern in their voices. Everyone was nervous about where the kingdom was headed from here.

Nautilus held up a paw to silence his citizens. They all quieted themselves at once. "Thank you for gathering here so quickly," Nautilus began. His voice rang clearly across the empire. "I wish that my first speech to you was under better circumstances. With great sadness, I must inform you that King Delta, my father, is no longer with us."

The empire bowed their heads mournfully.

Nautilus' crown glimmered in the rising sun. "Although I haven't lived here for very long, I know how respected my father was," he continued grimly. "It won't be easy to follow in his pawsteps, and live up to his greatness. I still have a lot to prove to the empire. Many of you doubt if I'm ready to become king. But I promise you that I'll be the best leader I can. No voice will go unheard in my reign, and no decision will be made unless in benefits our pack in full. I'll prove my worth to each of you, and show how much I care. The empire will see for itself that my words are not in vain."

Nautilus lifted himself taller. "We don't have to fear the future," he continued. "Not when we stand as one. Whatever lies ahead, we'll get through it together. We're Water Wolves, as resilient as the ocean itself. There's nothing we can't do with paws united." Bright beams of sun shone directly on Nautilus, turning his pelt gold. "It's time we begin a new chapter for the Water Pack. Together, as one, we will become stronger than ever before!"

The empire was silent for a moment.

Then—

"King Nautilus! King Nautilus! King Nautilus!" The empire erupted into cheer, chanting his name over and over again, so loudly that their voices could be heard from above the waves.

Nautilus watched his empire in awe, beginning to cry tears of joy. *I did it,* he thought. *I actually did it. I've finally become the wolf I'm meant to be.* He released all his emotion in one great, victorious howl, uniting his voice with the cheers of the Water Wolves.

Despite his overwhelming joy, Nautilus couldn't push away one dark thought that kept swirling through his mind. Where was Benthos, what was he planning, and when would he strike?

CHAPTER 17

As Nautilus swam through the ocean, dark clouds churned above the waves. He could sense the powerful winds that zipped through the sky. A storm was approaching.

Nautilus swam faster. Although he was reluctant to tell his friends the truth, Nautilus knew that it was best to get it over with. Aurora and Ember needed to know that Nautilus was king of the Water Pack now... and that he wouldn't have time to see them again for moons.

Nautilus eyed his bracelet sadly as he swam. Life had changed so much since he started his adventure. Part of Nautilus wished that things could go back to how they were. But Nautilus had commitments to see through, and promises to uphold.

As Nautilus swam through the coral reef that surrounded Emora Island, rain began to smack against the waves, causing the ocean roof to be alive with bubbles. A powerful current lashed at Nautilus' dark blue fur. He looked around nervously. There were no sea creatures in sight, and Nautilus guessed that they were all taking shelter until the storm passed.

Maybe it was a bad idea to come here alone, Nautilus realized. *I should have accepted Wave's company when she offered it.* He shook his head. *No. Saying goodbye to my friends is something that I need to do alone. I made the right choice, and I'll be back in the empire before the worst of the storm hits.*

Nautilus was unable to comfort himself, though. His fur bristled and his heartbeat was fast. Nautilus could sense that something was wrong, although he had no idea what. *It's just nerves about upsetting my friends,* he told himself. *Everything is fine.*

In a cascade of bubbles, Nautilus lifted his head above the swirling water. Rain immediately splashed into his eyes and splattered on his snout. Wind buffeted his soaked fur, making him shiver. Uncomfortable, Nautilus paddled to the shore of Emora Island, eager to find shelter.

He heaved himself out of the ocean, feeling weighted down by his sodden pelt. Nautilus quickly shook out his fur, causing droplets to fly in every direction. He then raced to the heart of the island while sand squelched beneath his paws. Before long, Nautilus was sheltered by the jungle trees. Wind groaned in the distance, but was thankfully unable to reach him. Nautilus let out a sigh of relief. He paused for a moment to catch his breath, then pushed through the foliage, heading deeper into the jungle.

It was strangely silent on the island. Normally, Nautilus would have heard his friends laughing, chatting, or working by now. Aurora and Ember must be sheltering until the storm passed, just like the creatures of the sea. Nothing to worry about.

Parrots glided beneath the canopy of leaves, squawking as Nautilus trudged to the camp. "Hello?" he called out. "Aurora? Ember? It's me. Nautilus. I, uh, have something to tell you." No response. "Guys? Can you hear me?"

Nautilus' pawsteps faltered. A strong scent wafted toward him, making him gag. It was a rancid, awful smell, one that made his head reel. "What in Elementa?" he spluttered through watering eyes. Had Ember attempted to cook something and accidentally lit it on fire?

Nautilus paused for a moment, coughing. It took every morsel of his self-control to wander closer to the camp. The scent grew stronger and stronger with every step he took. Nautilus found himself pushing through a veil of smoke as he neared the last of the jungle's trees.

"Guys?" Nautilus tried again. "Are you okay?" He suddenly halted. Terror exploded through him.

The treehouse his friends built had burned to the ground. Broken branches and tufts of fur were scattered throughout the meadow. Droplets of blood covered the scorched blades of grass. Nautilus nearly collapsed. "Aurora!" he called frantically. "Ember!

Answer me! Please!" All was silent for a dreadful moment. Nautilus couldn't stop himself from thinking the worse. Then—

"Mmph!" came a muffled voice, somewhere in the distance. "Mmph! Mrph!"

Nautilus weakly stumbled toward the source of the noise. His heart was pounding so fiercely that he thought it would explode. "Hello?" Nautilus whimpered.

"Mmph!" a voice answered.

"Mrph!" another voice said.

What in Elementa was going on here? Nautilus realized that the sounds were coming from behind a large boulder. With a shuddering breath, he crept to see the other side, dreading what he would find.

It was worse than Nautilus had imagined. Aurora and Ember were slumped on the ground, chained up and unable to move. Aurora's wings were painfully tied together in a mass of feathers. Ember had a terrible gash on his shoulder. Both of their snouts were chained shut, and their eyes were wide with horror.

Nautilus nearly fainted. "Hang on!" he cried. "I'll help you. Don't move." Nautilus frantically reached a paw toward Ember, wanting to free him first since he had the worst injuries. But when he did, Ember shook his head rapidly. "What's wrong?" Nautilus asked.

"Numph!" Ember cried. "Mmph!"

Aurora repeatedly lashed her head in the direction of the ocean. "Wrmph!"

Nautilus was completely weirded out and utterly terrified at the same time. "You want me to go?" he asked in a trembling voice.

They both nodded like their lives depended on it. Suddenly, their eyes filled with fear.

Nautilus was suddenly struck. The blow was so powerful that he was knocked to the ground. Nautilus slid across the wet grass. Before he came to a complete halt, he was kicked in the ribs, and tumbled back. Pain seared through Nautilus in an agonizing wave.

Before he could stand, something pounced on him. Nautilus tried to break away, but it was no use. His attacker was too powerful. "Finally," the wolf sneered in a venomous voice. "We thought that you'd never show up."

Nautilus twisted his head to face his opponent. He gasped. It was a Fire Wolf! She had a dark red pelt and gleaming, orange eyes. Her fangs were bared as she let out a slow, menacing growl.

Three other Fire Wolves emerged from the smoke and shadows, prowling closer. They looked just as hostile as the wolf pinning Nautilus. One Fire Wolf even had a pelt that was completely on fire. The newcomers looked wild, brash, unpredictable, and undeniably dangerous.

These are the Fire Wolves Aurora told me about! Nautilus remembered with a jolt of fear. *They found us. But what do they want? Why did they attack us? We did nothing to them, so what's their motivation for doing all this damage?* Nautilus gulped. *And why does it sound like they were hoping I'd come?*

The answer to his last question became painfully clear. The haze of smoke swirled in front of Nautilus once more. Shining, yellow eyes were the first to appear, followed by the rest of the massive wolf. Dread crashed down on Nautilus. It was Benthos.

"Hello, Brother," he growled in a dangerous voice. "Or, should I say, Your Highness?"

"Benthos," Nautilus snarled, struggling to breathe under the weight of the Fire Wolf. "I demand that you stop this at once."

Benthos smirked. "I don't take orders from you," he chuckled. "I heard all about your rise to kingship from my spies, but it changes nothing. The throne is mine, and mine alone. You were merely keeping it warm for me until I could deal with you properly."

Aurora and Ember looked shocked to hear of Nautilus' kingship. They stared at him in absolute bewilderment.

An evil smile slithered across Benthos' face. "I'm pleased to say that my plan worked better than expected," he continued slyly.

"*Our* plan," the Fire Wolf pinning Nautilus corrected. "If you hadn't come crawling to us for help, you would never have succeeded in terminating the Water Pack king."

Nautilus' eyes widened.

Benthos flashed her a hostile smile. "Yes, Flare," he said through clenched teeth. "Forgive me for not acknowledging our wondrous partnership sooner."

Flare lashed her tail. At her command, the three other Fire Wolves moved closer to Benthos, surrounding him on all sides. "We will eliminate the king as discussed," Flare told Benthos. "Now, I expect you to uphold your end of the bargain. There will be *unsightly* consequences if you refuse to give us what you promised."

Benthos grinned. "No need to get worked up," he said pleasantly. "I intend to give you what I promised. It's the least I can do in exchange for you taking my nuisance of a brother off my paws." Benthos unhooked a woven pouch from the sash he wore. He tossed it at the two smallest Fire Wolves, who fought over it in a fit of growling. Benthos laughed.

"Blaze! Spark! Knock it off!" Flare screamed at them.

Spark managed to bite Blaze's paw, who pulled back with a yelp. Spark then snatched up the pouch and dragged it away from her sister. Spark dumped out the contents of the pouch then studied them with a greedy expression. "It's all here," Spark confirmed after a few seconds. "Fifty pieces of Blue Elemental Heart."

"You sold me out?" Nautilus demanded with a furious glare at Benthos.

"Of course I did," he responded breezily. "How could I not? Partnering with these Fire Wolves was the perfect plan. They were seeking to capture Ember, Aurora, Sandstorm and you, Brother, while I was looking to get rid of you myself." Benthos took a dangerous step forward. "The enemy of my enemy is my friend, as the saying goes. It was a joy working with these Fire Wolves to destroy you and your lowly friends."

Nautilus was furious. "Don't think this is over," he threatened.

Benthos laughed. "Oh, I certainly do," he retorted. "So long, Brother. I have a throne to claim and an empire to conquer." Benthos' eyes narrowed into slits. "More importantly, I have a short-lived king to wipe from the memories of my servants. I'll make sure no wolf remembers you, Nautilus. You'll be a goner in more ways than one."

Benthos turned around and prowled away. He vanished into the shadows, leaving Nautilus behind forever.

Flare watched Benthos go with a loathing glare. "Good riddance," she spat, once Benthos was out of earshot. Flare turned to the Fire Wolf with the pelt that was constantly in flames. "Scorch! Make yourself useful and guard the prisoners."

Scorch rolled his eyes and made his way to Aurora and Ember, leaving a trail of flames in the grass. Ember watched him approach with furious, hateful eyes. Scorch gave him a glare that was just as angry. "Can I kill him?" he asked Flare.

"No," Flare growled. "Ember is not to be harmed until we return him to Father."

"Return?" Nautilus asked.

Flare painfully dug her claws into Nautilus' fur. "Silence!" she screamed. "You have no more authority, Water Wolf. From now on, you do whatever I say, and obey the commands of Princess Flare!"

"What about us?" Spark demanded. Flames exploded out of her nose when she let out an angry breath. "We're just as royal as you are!"

"You're more like a royal pain," Blaze huffed.

Spark immediately leapt at her sister and tackled her to the ground, snarling. Blaze viciously bit Spark on the ear. Scorch laughed hysterically.

Aurora looked mortified. Ember let out a sigh while closing his eyes, unable to believe that this was actually happening.

"Hold on," Nautilus told Flare. At her glare, he quickly added, "I just want to know one thing. If you're royalty, does that mean King Inferno is your father?"

"Obviously," Scorch sneered.

Nautilus couldn't believe it. He gazed up at Flare in wonder. "Listen to me, all of you," Nautilus told the Fire Wolves. "I have to tell you something."

Flare's pelt bristled furiously. "Who said I gave you permission to speak?" she spat.

"This is important," Nautilus interjected. He felt far less afraid of the Fire Wolves now that he knew who they were. "The five of us aren't so different. The truth is, Ash, your mother, is my mother too. We're all half-siblings."

Silence fell over the island. Nobody moved.

"Didn't you hear me?" Nautilus asked nervously. He gazed at Flare. "You, Spark, Blaze, Scorch and I are all half-siblings."

Flare slashed Nautilus' cheek with brutal force. "You're lying," she growled. "Ash had no other pups than us. Especially not with some Water Wolf fool."

"Yeah!" Spark screamed. "If you're trying to trick us, it won't work."

"The last thing we need is another sibling," Scorch snorted. He glanced at Ember distastefully. "Having Ember as our rocks-for-brains brother is already more than enough."

"Mmph!" Aurora gasped in alarm.

"What?!" Nautilus cried. "Ember is... what?!"

"Our brother," Scorch repeated. "Didn't he ever tell you he was a prince?"

All eyes turned to stare at Ember. He looked mortified. Ember's worst nightmare was unfolding around him, and he was helpless to change a thing.

Nautilus met Ember's gaze, breathing fast. "I can't believe it," he choked out. "You're my brother. We're... we're siblings. No. It can't be true. It can't... we can't be... no..."

Ember looked beyond afraid, past the point of shocked. He looked... broken. Something in his eyes was no longer the same. It was like he was only a shell of his former self.

"Enough of this!" Flare shrieked. "Blaze! Spark! Cage this Water Wolf. Scorch! Load Ember and the Sky Wolf onto the ship. We've been keeping Father waiting far too long." She released Nautilus, pushing him toward Blaze and Spark. He wanted to fight, but knew that it was hopeless. He was overpowered, outnumbered, and outsmarted. Keeping his head low, Nautilus reluctantly followed his captors.

Flare turned her malevolent eyes onto Ember. She slowly walked toward him, causing a dark shadow to fall over his fur. "It's time to take you back home... Brother."

CHAPTER 18

Nautilus fell into a puddle of mud when Blaze and Spark roughly pushed him toward the cage. Before he could stand, Blaze clamped her fangs around Nautilus' scruff and painfully yanked him to his paws. "Hurry up," she snarled. "Father doesn't like to be kept waiting."

Nautilus nervously eyed the ship up ahead. It was truly fit for royalty. It was decorated from top to bottom with glistening volcanic rocks, so tightly placed together that they almost looked like scales. It created the illusion that the ship was a living, reptilian creature, as black as the darkest night. The blood-red sails thrashed wildly in the wind, while the stern of the ship bobbed up and down in the violent waves.

Nautilus glanced over his shoulder.

Aurora and Ember were trudging toward the ship in silence. Ember looked shaken, while Aurora had a murderous look on her face. Her green eyes were livid and the scar on her snout made her look twice as intimidating. If Aurora's muzzle wasn't chained shut, she probably would have bitten someone by now. Her tied wings twitched, as if she was imagining herself swooping into battle to protect her mate and friend.

Nautilus found himself wondering if Flare had made a mistake when she ordered her siblings to remove the chains on Aurora's and Ember's paws. The decision was made so that Aurora and Ember would walk themselves to the far side of the island. However, seeing how fierce Aurora looked, Nautilus couldn't help but think that the decision was foolish on Flare's part.

"Keep moving," Spark abruptly snarled, stomping on Nautilus' sensitive tail. He gasped in pain. Although he hated submitting to these tyrannical Fire Wolves, Nautilus had enough sense to avoid fighting back. He silently walked into the cage that rested on the deck of the ship, his head lowered in shame, wishing that this was a nightmare he'd wake up from soon.

Blaze slammed the cage door shut. She lifted one of her paws and allowed it to ignite on fire. With a ghastly sizzle, Blaze placed her paw on the lock, melting it. Nautilus was trapped.

Spark let out a wicked laugh. "Oh, how the mighty have fallen," she sneered. "Aren't you supposed to be some powerful king? What's wrong with you?" Spark pounced on the cage's side, causing it to rattle violently. Nautilus flinched, feeling like the lowest sea slug in the world.

"Blaze! Spark! Get your sorry tails down here!" Flare abruptly called.

The two sisters rolled their eyes at the same time. Reluctantly, they left Nautilus behind, then made their way off the ship. Nautilus crept forward to peer down at the shore. Whatever happened next, at least he wouldn't face it alone.

Ember was cruelly ushered onto the ship by Blaze and Spark, who clawed his pelt and threw insults at him without ceasing. Ember looked too mortified to do anything but stumble forward weakly.

Spark opened the door of the cage closest to Nautilus. Blaze shoved Ember inside. He tripped on his way in, landing heavily on his already wounded shoulder. The bleeding became even worse. Blaze and Spark laughed as they locked the cage door.

"Ember!" Nautilus cried, pressing himself against the bars. "Are you okay?"

"Silence!" Flare growled. Her orange eyes glowed ghoulishly in the storm as she prowled onto the ship. She glared at Blaze and Spark. "Don't just stand there! Lift the anchor. Get ready to sail to the Fire Pack Dominion."

"What about the Sky Wolf?" Blaze asked.

"Scorch is loading her on now," Flare responded impatiently. "Now get to work! Immediately!"

Blaze and Spark slithered out of sight, making their way to the far side of the ship. Flare gave her brothers a brief scowl before she headed to the front of the deck. It was just Nautilus and Ember now.

Nautilus reached a paw through the bars of the two cages and gently shook Ember. He was still on his side, his eyes shut tightly. "Hey," Nautilus whispered anxiously. "Are you okay? Oh, you can't answer. Never mind." Nautilus fidgeted with his bracelet. "I have an idea. Don't move. I'm going to melt away the chains on your muzzle so you can talk."

Just before Nautilus transformed into a Fire Wolf, a furious scream erupted from the shore.

Ember, finding sudden strength, heaved himself to his paws to see what was happening. Nautilus fearfully gazed through the bars. Something was wrong.

Scorch was facing off with Aurora. The two wolves growled furiously, their eyes bright with rage. "I command you to keep moving!" Scorch screamed at her. His flaming pelt burned fiercer in his anger, causing the entire beach to glow red.

Aurora held her ground, glaring defiantly at Scorch. She didn't move, not even a muscle.

"Scorch!" Flare suddenly called from the front of the ship. "Hurry up or I'm leaving you here!"

Scorch gave Aurora a seething look. "Get on the ship right now," he snarled dangerously, "or I'll turn you into a pile of ash."

Aurora didn't flinch. *She isn't backing down,* Nautilus realized. *What is she thinking? Aurora doesn't stand a chance against Scorch while she's chained up like that. She'll be killed!*

Ember looked horrified. He whipped around to face Nautilus. *Do something!* the look in Ember's eyes screamed. *Make it stop!*

"Aurora!" Nautilus cried. "Don't! This isn't a battle you can win!"

Aurora ignored him. She extended her claws, bracing herself to fight.

Scorch grinned maliciously. "Time's up, Sky Wolf," he hissed. "You're mine." Scorch exploded to Aurora, ready to burn her alive. Aurora dodged his flaming paws at the last moment. She instinctively reached out a paw to strike Scorch, then immediately pulled back. How could Aurora fight an enemy that she couldn't touch?

Scorch rushed at Aurora again, moving faster than before. Aurora tumbled out of his way—but she hadn't been fast enough. Scorch managed to snag a few of her feathers as he zoomed past her. They immediately burned to cinders. What would happen to Aurora if Scorch managed to land a full-on blow?

Ember desperately threw himself against his cage, urgently trying to break free. He was about to watch his mate die.

Aurora hit the ground with a thud. Scorch loomed over her with a triumphant smirk. "So long, Sky Wolf," he sneered. Scorch reared up on his back paws, then thrust his front paws down to Aurora.

"No!" Nautilus screamed.

As fast as lightning, Aurora twisted around so that Scorch's paws landed on the chains tying her wings. The silver immediately turned red with a terrible hiss. Scorch stumbled back, looking startled.

With all her strength, Aurora unfolded her wings, causing the melting chains to pull apart. They fell to the ground, landing near her paws.

Aurora was free!

Scorch let out a furious roar. He leapt at Aurora, but before the two wolves collided, Aurora lifted into the stormy sky. Scorch lost his balance and toppled to the ground. With a livid snarl, he lifted himself to his paws and whipped to face the ship. "Flare!" he screamed. "The Sky Wolf! She got free!"

Aurora swooped to Ember and Nautilus, landing in front of their cages. Ember was so relieved that he looked like he was about to collapse. He stumbled closer to Aurora, and the two wolves held paws while gazing into each other's eyes.

Seriously?! They were being lovey now? "Guys!" Nautilus cried. "There's no time!"

Aurora immediately snapped out of it. She hooked her claws around the lock on Ember's cage. Aurora tugged with all her might, but it wouldn't break.

"Watch out!" Nautilus cried.

A fireball abruptly whooshed toward Aurora. She ducked her head at the last possible second, dodging it safely.

Flare let out a wild scream as she ran to Aurora, launching fireball after fireball from her paws. Blaze and Spark abruptly appeared, sending blasts of fire at Aurora. It was absolute mayhem. Nautilus and Ember were nearly burned alive themselves.

Left with no other choice, Aurora lifted into the stormy sky. Flare refused to back down. She sent a storm of fireballs at Aurora, hoping to knock her straight out of the air. Aurora immediately turned around and flew away—leaving her friends behind.

"Aurora!" Nautilus cried. "Get help! Please!"

Ember watched Aurora go with round, hopeless eyes.

The Sky Wolf disappeared behind a dark storm cloud and vanished from sight. She was gone.

Not a single wolf moved. All was silent for a long, long time, as if the world itself was holding its breath. Nautilus turned to warily gaze at Flare. Her face was twisted with rage, and her pelt rose and fell with every sharp, furious breath she took.

"NO!" Flare shrieked, releasing all her anger in one booming word.

Blaze and Spark flinched. They slowly slunk away, creeping to a further part of the ship. Nautilus held his breath, wanting to avoid catching Flare's attention at all costs.

Scorch suddenly scrambled onto the deck. Flare immediately shot a fireball at him. "Ouch!" Scorch yelped. He gave his flaming pelt a shake. "Rude."

"You!" Flare spat. She ominously prowled toward Scorch. "You ruined everything! You let the Sky Wolf escape!"

Scorch shrugged. "So what?" he sneered.

Flare looked like she was about to explode with anger. "I promised Father that I would retrieve Ember, the Water Wolf, *and* the Sky Wolf!" she snarled. "Don't you understand what you've done by letting that Sky Wolf escape?"

Scorch shook his head, clueless.

"Father will see me as a failure!" Flare cried. "I... I've never disappointed him before. This is the first mission he gave me where I didn't succeed. Once he discovers the truth, he'll... he'll..." Flare looked sick, swaying on her paws.

Ember watched his sister without moving. Was that understanding in his eyes?

Scorch flicked his ear nonchalantly. "That's your problem," he heartlessly told Flare. "It's no fur off my back if Father gets rid of you. The less siblings I have, the better. I'm done with you all." Scorch pushed past Flare and headed into one of the cabins, slamming the door behind him.

Nautilus stiffened, realizing that he was alone with his half-siblings on deck. Flare looked at Ember briefly with a scowl on her face, before turning around and prowling away.

Before long, the sound of clanging filled the silence as Blaze and Spark lifted the anchor. The ship floated away from the shore of Emora Island, heading deeper into the untamed ocean.

Ember didn't move as he watched the island become smaller and smaller, until they could no longer see it on the horizon. Nautilus wished he could comfort his half-brother, but he knew his efforts would be in vain. Ember had lost Aurora, his home, and his freedom all on the same day.

Could things possibly get any worse from here?

As the ship violently swayed in the deadly waves, Nautilus had a feeling that things were indeed going to get worse. A lot worse. They were heading to the

Fire Pack Dominion, and right into King Inferno's claws. This was truly the beginning of the end.

Please, Aurora, Nautilus called out, as if she could hear his thoughts. *Do something to make this nightmare end. Ember and I need your help now more than ever.* Nautilus hung his head. He knew in his heart that no one could hear him, and that nobody was coming to save them.

Nautilus and Ember were on their own now. If they wanted to get out of this alive, they needed to fight for their very survival. There was no room for error. One wrong step, and they would be done for.

Nautilus felt fierce determination burn inside him when he saw Ember. His half-brother looked miserable and entirely defeated. *I'm King Nautilus of the Water Pack Empire,* he reminded himself. *And I'll fight until my last breath to protect those who need it most. Aurora may be long gone, but it doesn't mean that all hope is lost. I'll find a way to get us through this. I'll be my own hero, and I'll make things right. No matter what it takes, our journey will continue. This won't be the end. I promise it.*

Nautilus reached his paw through the bars and gently placed it on Ember's shoulder. "We're going to get through this," he told his brother. "Now hold still. I'm going to melt those chains on your snout. It's time we come up with a plan."

CHAPTER 19

The ship swayed violently in the raging sea as Nautilus transformed into a Fire Wolf. The metal bars underneath his paws began to heat up, but to his disappointment, they didn't melt. *Of course the cage is heat resistant,* Nautilus thought bitterly. *My half-siblings aren't as dim as they appear.*

Nautilus moved his scorching paw through the tangle of bars. Ember flinched slightly, but kept still as Nautilus cautiously melted away the chains. The silver became glowing red, and before long, the chains fell off Ember's snout.

Well, maybe they're still a bit dim, Nautilus thought. *They didn't expect Ember to be able to melt his chains, since he doesn't have an elemental power. But did they seriously think I wouldn't help him do it? Surely Benthos told them I was a hybrid.*

Ember rubbed his snout with his paw, wincing at the pain.

"Are you okay?" Nautilus asked.

To his absolute bewilderment, Ember gave him a furious growl. "No," he shouted. "I am *not* okay. This is an absolute nightmare—and I can't wake up from this mess! Nautilus, I hate you."

"Whoa," Nautilus said sarcastically, taking a step back. "Don't get your tail in a knot. What in Elementa did I do?"

Ember slammed his front paws against the cage wall, snarling. "What *didn't* you do?" he spat. "You took everything from me! You don't deserve any of the gifts you have. Everything you have should me mine, you pathetic lump of fur!"

Nautilus rolled his eyes. "Are you still mad about our differences in elemental powers?" he asked. "It's not my fault I have three, and it certainly isn't my fault that you have none. Don't blame me for what destiny planned." Nautilus transformed back into a Water Wolf, hoping that his familiar appearance would calm Ember down. However, it only seemed to make him angrier.

"Oh, you must think you've matured so much," Ember sneered. "But I know who you really are, Nautilus. You're a coward who's scared of your own shadow. Don't think for a moment that you're some wise king. You can't even see what's right under your snout."

Nautilus kept quiet, meeting Ember's gaze without flinching.

"It wasn't destiny that ruined my life," Ember hissed in a low, dangerous voice. His orange eyes were murderous. "It was you, Nautilus. It was you from the very start. I finally see that now." Ember tightened his grip around the bars. "If you had never been born, Mother would have loved me and my siblings. She would have stayed in the Fire Pack, but thanks to you, her heart was elsewhere. That must be why she left us. Left me."

Ember's pelt rose and fell with every sharp, furious breath he took. "My father only became the monster he is now because Mother disappeared," he continued lividly. "If it wasn't for you, Nautilus, he never would have tried to end my life. I wouldn't have had to run away from the Fire Pack. I should have still had a home. A family. But now I have nothing, and it's all your fault!"

Ember violently slammed himself against the cage, trying to break through so he could tear Nautilus to shreds.

Nautilus held his ground and bared his fangs. "You need to get a grip, Ember!" he shouted. "This isn't you. What would Aurora think if she could see you now?"

"Aurora isn't here!" Ember screamed. His voice was filled with anguish. "The one wolf who cared about me is gone. And if we never came to this stupid ocean for you, then she would still be with me now! Aurora and I would be together, safe, and happy."

Nautilus lashed his tail. "You aren't thinking straight," he told Ember. "I understand you're afraid of going back to the Fire Pack. I know that you've suffered a lot. I see where you're coming from. But you need to fight your anger before it consumes you, Ember. I'm scared of the wolf you're becoming."

Ember looked away, clenching his jaw.

Nautilus held up his wrist to show Ember his bracelet. "Remember this?" he gently asked. "You worked hard to make this for me. Aurora told me that you wanted to make me happy by surprising me with my first ever birthday gift." Nautilus fondly looked at his bracelet. "I've never taken it off since that day. Whenever I felt afraid or alone in the Water Pack, I looked at my bracelet, and I was reminded of you and Aurora—my friends."

Ember suddenly reached through the bars and snatched the bracelet. He yanked it off Nautilus' wrist, then pulled it into his cage. Ember viciously stomped on the bracelet with his paw. It snapped in two.

Nautilus' entire face filled with despair. He was so stunned that he couldn't even breathe for a moment. "My bracelet," he choked out. "You broke it."

Ember gave Nautilus a cold glare. "You and I are no longer friends," he said, "and it's all because of your selfishness. You did this to yourself." Ember turned around and stalked to the far side of his cage. He sat down with his back turned to Nautilus, shivering as a cold wind tore past the ship.

Heartbroken, Nautilus pawed the remains of his bracelet closer, hoping that he could somehow mend it back together. The painting of Ember had been severed from the depictions of Nautilus and Aurora. The sight made Nautilus whimper. How could things have gone so wrong, so quickly?

Without warning, a shrill howl filled the silence. "Prepare for landing," Flare commanded from the front of the ship. "Immediately!"

Blaze, Spark, and Scorch appeared and reluctantly began to work. Nautilus looked past his half-siblings to stare across the ocean. The blistering wind lashed at his fur and caused his eyes to water.

Up ahead was an enormous, black island. It was jagged and filled with spikes everywhere Nautilus looked. Streams of gooey lava illuminated the darkness with an eerie red glow. Cinders floated through the sky like grey snow, while a haze of smoke swirled through the land.

This was the Fire Pack Dominion. As Nautilus stared at the nightmarish land, he began to tremble from ears to tail. *Why do I have a feeling that this is the place where I'm going to die?* he thought with a gulp.

The Fire Pack slowly crept closer and closer by the second. The island cast a long shadow over the tiny ship as it floated to the black shore. Nautilus' eyes widened. His instincts screamed for him to run, hurry, and flee as fast as he could. But Nautilus was trapped. He was as helpless as a fish in a net. There was no possibility of escape. No chance of freedom. No hope.

Nautilus transformed into a Fire Wolf, hoping that this pack would be more merciful if he looked like them. "Gross!" Spark shrieked when she saw Nautilus' transformation. "Benthos was right. You really are a hybrid. That's so disgusting. I hope father throws you into the volcano first." Nautilus hung his head in shame.

With a loud crunching sound, the ship landed on the black, pebble-filled shore of the Fire Pack Dominion. The doors of the cages were opened, and Nautilus and Ember were led off the ship. Nautilus was tempted to make a run for the ocean, but didn't dare. Flare was watching the two wolves with eyes as sharp as daggers. She wouldn't let another prisoner escape on her watch again. Not after losing Aurora so carelessly.

Ember's paws shook as he was forced to walk deeper into the island. Nautilus shared his brother's fear as he crept slowly behind him. They were surrounded by Blaze, Spark, Scorch, and Flare, who closed the two wolves in on all sides. From the shadows, Nautilus saw flickers of movement, and realized that Fire Wolves were stalking them from the darkness.

Nautilus' fur stood on end. This place was awful. He felt grateful that he didn't have to grow up here, and he no longer wondered why Ember was prone to being so hostile. The Fire Pack was so miserable that it would shrivel the heart of any wolf who lived here. Now Nautilus understood Ember's misery.

Nautilus slowly moved closer to Ember. Once he was close enough, he whispered, "I'm sorry."

Ember's eyes widened. They then filled with overwhelming sorrow. Ember was about to whisper something back, but Flare shot a warning fireball over their heads before he could speak. "Silence!" Flare demanded through clenched teeth.

Nautilus and Ember continued on without another word. Before long, they reached the heart of the island, where lakes of gurgling lava were strewn across the black earth. Wolves in dark cloaks silently wandered from place to place. When they saw Flare and her royal siblings approach, they immediately darted away to hide in the shadows.

"This way," Flare ordered. "King Inferno awaits." She led them up a steep volcanic hill. Something huge and shiny caught Nautilus' attention, and he realized that there was an obsidian throne suspended above a pit of lava. His throat felt dry. This was truly the stuff of nightmares.

Ember looked traumatized as they continued to trudge upward. Then, he just... stopped.

"Uh, Flare?" Blaze called. "I think Ember broke."

Flare immediately turned around with a frightening glower. "Keep moving *now*," she told Ember in a venomous voice. When he remained still, Flare shot a fireball near his paws. "Didn't you hear me? I said, *move!*" Still, Ember held his ground. What in Elementa was he thinking? This was no time to disobey!

"Come on, Ember," Nautilus urged quietly. "Do what they say."

Something in Ember's eyes snapped. "No!" he abruptly screamed. His voice echoed through the silent island. "I've lived my entire life in fear because of them. But no more! I'm sick of being afraid. I've had enough of running and hiding. It's time I take a stand!" Ember suddenly rushed at Flare. He tackled her to the ground. The two wolves clawed and thrashed wildly.

Nautilus was so shocked that he couldn't move for a moment. Blaze, Spark and Scorch watched the fight in surprise. "Don't just stand there you fools!" Flare roared as Ember bit her shoulder. Flare slashed Ember's muzzle. "Get him!"

The three Fire Wolves immediately threw themselves into the battle. *They'll kill him!* Nautilus realized in horror. Without thinking, he ran to Scorch and crashed into his side. Pain rushed through Nautilus when he touched Scorch's flaming pelt, but thanks to his Fire Wolf form, the damage was minimal.

Caught off balance, Scorch tumbled sideways. He slid toward a lake of lava—then fell right into the burning depths. Nautilus' breath caught in his throat. Just before he assumed the worst, Scorch's head surfaced. He looked furious, yet completely unharmed. Scorch paddled back to land, struggling to move in the thick, gooey lava. It would take a few minutes before he escaped.

Nautilus rushed back to the fight. Ember was on the ground, suffering blow after blow from Flare, Blaze, and Spark. "Leave him alone!" Nautilus screamed. He threw himself at Flare and dug his claws into her shoulder.

In one swift movement, Flare dislodged Nautilus and slammed him against the ground. "Forget Ember for now!" she told her sisters. "Let's finish off this hybrid. Father didn't ask for him alive." Nautilus' eyes widened.

Ember suddenly knocked Blaze and Spark off their paws, then hurried over to Flare. Just before she harmed Nautilus, Ember viciously sunk his fangs into her leg. Flare let out a screech of pain, buckling to the ground.

For a moment, it was just Nautilus and Ember standing. "You need to leave," Ember hurriedly told Nautilus. "Reclaim your throne and be the wolf you're meant to be. Hurry!"

"What about you?" Nautilus demanded. "I can't leave you here!"

Blaze and Spark were rising to their paws. Scorch was almost at the edge of the lava lake. Time was running out.

"You need to!" Ember screamed. "Do this for me, Nautilus. Let me make up for my cruelty. I hate myself for what I said to you—for what I did. I want to do something good before I meet my fate. Please. Go!"

Nautilus hesitated, his eyes wide.

"Go!" Ember screamed again.

The fear in Ember's voice was enough to make Nautilus give in. He began to run—run faster than he ever had before. With thunderous snarls, Blaze and Spark pursued Nautilus. Ember threw himself in their way, sacrificing his freedom for Nautilus'.

Flare shot a fireball at Nautilus, but missed. "Get him!" she cried. "Packmates! Anyone! Make sure that hybrid doesn't escape!" Flare attempted to rise to her paws, but immediately collapsed again. She let out a growl of anguish.

Nautilus wheezed and gasped for breath as he continued to rush to the shore. He didn't look back once—he couldn't bear to see an army of Fire Wolves chasing him, and he would have nightmares if he saw Ember being killed to save him.

Keep going. Faster. Faster! Don't look back. Hurry. Keep going. Run. Run. Nautilus coughed. His paws felt like heavy boulders. And yet he kept running. Nautilus refused to let Ember's sacrifice be in vain. He would live on for the two of them.

After what felt like an eternity of running, the ocean finally came into view. Nautilus exploded toward the waves. He leapt through the air, transforming into a Water Wolf at the same time. Nautilus landed in the water with a massive splash. He immediately dove down to the deepest depths, hiding under the waves.

Nautilus was still and silent for a long, long time. His head was reeling. Adrenaline pumped through his veins. *I did it,* Nautilus thought shakily. *I escaped.* Nautilus buried his head in his webbed paws. *But Ember wasn't so lucky.* Guilt immediately ravaged his heart. *Why did I leave him there? I should have fought with Ember. We could have escaped the island together. Why didn't I do more?* Nautilus whimpered like a lost pup. *Even if I went back... it's probably already too late for Ember.*

Nautilus felt dizzy. He wrapped his tail around his body, pulling himself into a tight ball of fur. Nautilus was so rattled that, for a moment, he considered swimming away from Elementa forever. He could escape all his heartache and stress if he simply abandoned the continent. But Nautilus knew in his heart that he was stronger than that. *No. I can't give in to grief now. Ember wanted me to escape. I did this for him as well as for myself. If I was in Ember's position, I would have sacrificed myself, too. I did the right thing, despite how painful the choice was.*

With a shuddering breath, he moved his tail back and lifted himself off the sea floor. *This is no time for regrets,* Nautilus told himself. *Benthos is a monster and he needs to be stopped. Who knows what destruction he's already brought upon the Water Pack? It's probably worse than I can imagine.*

Nautilus lifted his head, forcing himself to be brave. *I'm the king of this ocean. If Benthos wants to harm my pack and my home, he'll have to go through me.* Nautilus hesitated for a moment, feeling somber and grim. He then glided through the water, heading back to the Water Pack Empire.

Get ready for me, Benthos, Nautilus thought. *It's time you and I settle our royal rivalry once and for all.*

CHAPTER 20

The ocean was eerily silent. Unnaturally still. There was no sign of life anywhere beneath the waves, as if every soul was hiding someplace unseen. Nautilus' heartbeat quickened. Up ahead was the empire, darkened in shadow. There was no movement, no noise, and no wolves.

What in Elementa happened? Nautilus wondered nervously. *Why is everything so silent now? What happened to the music, and all the cheerful Water Wolves? Is everyone all right?* Fear flowed through his veins. *What has Benthos done?*

Nautilus swam faster, feeling an untameable sense of urgency to reach his empire. Time was running out to protect the pack from Benthos' greedy claws. Nautilus needed to save his home before it was too late. He was the only one who could stand up to his brother. But would Nautilus survive the process?

The young king shook his head. *I must survive,* he told himself. *I need to be strong—not just for my empire and friends, but for myself, too. It's time I prove my worth to all of Elementa. I'm not the coward I used to be. Although I'm still afraid of failure, I no longer let that fear control me.*

Nautilus' eyes shimmered with determination. *I'm going to show Benthos how far I've come.*

The storm clouds on the surface slowly began to break apart. As Nautilus swam into the empire, a powerful red glow illuminated the ocean as the sun lowered behind the waves. Nautilus lifted himself taller as he paddled through the labyrinth of shimmering gold and silver towers. He swam to the castle with swift, confident strokes.

Despite his steady outward appearance, Nautilus was beginning to feel worried. He seemed to be the only Water Wolf in the entire world. The only trace of his packmates were brief flickers of movement from the shadows. Nautilus' ears flattened. What had driven his fellow Water Wolves into hiding?

"Look," came a soft, fragile whisper from the sidelines. "King Nautilus has returned. He's alive." A tiny pup emerged from the darkness, giving Nautilus a surprised look.

"King Nautilus is here?" came another whisper.

"Did someone say King Nautilus?" asked another.

The space around Nautilus soon became filled with stunned Water Wolves. They surrounded him with awed expressions, looking like they were staring at a ghost. Nautilus was silent for a moment, unsure of how to respond.

An elderly Water Wolf swam through the crowd. She halted and bowed a respectful distance in front of Nautilus. "Your Highness," she creaked. "Forgive me for speaking so openly, but where did you go? How are you still alive? Benthos told us you had been killed by a group of vicious Fire Wolves."

Anger rushed through Nautilus like a flaming wave. "My brother lied to you," he told the Water Wolves, his voice echoing through the deserted underwater streets of the empire. "I'm still alive, no thanks to him. Benthos tried to get rid of me so he could have the throne all to himself."

The crowd gasped, looking horrified.

"I need to find Benthos," Nautilus continued briskly. "Have any of you seen him lately?"

Each wolf appeared nervous. A bleak silence filled the area for a moment. "Benthos has been destroying the Royal Memorial with his own claws since he returned to the empire," a light green wolf explained. "He told the pack that his first act as king is to kill the past to let his future shine. It's terrible, King Nautilus. Benthos has been breaking every statue of his ancestors, leaving nothing behind."

"Benthos is a monster," a dark purple wolf spat. "I always knew he was bad, but I never expected him to start ordering the capture and imprisonment of innocent wolves."

"What?" Nautilus gasped.

"That's why the empire has gone into hiding," the dark purple wolf continued. "Benthos has sent guards to hunt down his own citizens, dragging them into the dungeons for reasons we don't know. At first, Benthos was only targeting the higher ranking wolves. Some royal advisors. A few nobles. He even went after guards, and captured Commander Wave." His fur bristled. "Now Benthos is going after us smaller wolves and we don't know why. You have to help us, Your Highness. You're the only one who can."

Nautilus nodded sternly. "Of course I'm going to help you," he told his packmates. "I'll fight to protect our empire until my last breath. Benthos isn't going to get away with his crimes. I promise." Nautilus' dark blue fur swayed in the cool current. "I'm going to challenge Benthos to a Battle of Power."

"With all due respect, King Nautilus, is this a fight you're sure you can win?" someone in the crowd asked. "Engaging in a Battle of Power is a fight to the death. Only one of you can come out alive. What will happen to us if Benthos is the victor?"

"I won't let Benthos win," Nautilus calmly told the Water Wolves.

Despite his reassuring tone, fear thundered through his veins. Nautilus was no brute. He was a bit on the smaller side and had a soft and cuddly appearance. Meanwhile, Benthos was a massive wolf who had strength rippling beneath his fur. Could Nautilus possibly win in a battle against his adopted brother?

"Stay here," Nautilus told the crowd, "and stay safe. This is a fight I want my pack to have no role in." They nodded and started to slip back into the shadows. "So long, everyone. Hopefully, when we meet again, the empire will be a safer place." Nautilus continued to swim through the empty empire, struggling to keep his heart from racing.

The gigantic golden castle appeared in the distance. It glittered nauseatingly as the dark red sunlight hit it, making Nautilus feel sick. As he swam closer, the massive shadow of the looming fortress fell on Nautilus' pelt. He shuddered, feeling suddenly cold. There were the heads and limbs of statues everywhere, littering the courtyard. Nautilus' breathing quickened as he silently swam above the stone remains that had once depicted his royal ancestors. He nearly cried out with despair when he saw the stone head of King Delta—his father.

Benthos is worse than I ever could have imagined, Nautilus thought, clenching his paws into fists. *I refuse to let that sorry excuse of a wolf sit on my throne. Benthos will pay for all his actions. He won't terrorize my empire for a moment longer!*

Nautilus stormed into the castle. "BENTHOS!" he roared. Nautilus' voice sliced through the empty corridors. "Your time is up! I'll make you regret hurting my friends and empire!" Nautilus rushed to the throne room, knowing in his heart that he would find Benthos there. He threw open the doors, growling fiercely.

Benthos was lounging on the throne without a care in the world. He lazily tossed a pawful of seaweed crisps into his mouth, smirking. "Oh, hello, Brother," Benthos sneered, adjusting King Delta's crown from atop his head. "You're still alive, are you? Funny. I knew those Fire Wolves were more useless than they were letting on. Oh well. I'll just have to shred you with my own claws." Benthos yawned, purposefully showing off his razor-sharp fangs.

Nautilus' fur wildly bristled, making him look twice his size. "You and I are going to settle our royal rivalry once and for all!" he shouted. "I challenge you to a Battle of Power!"

Benthos was silent for a moment. He then... laughed. It was a mocking, terrible sound, one that slithered through Nautilus' ears. "Are you sure that's what you want?" Benthos sneered dangerously. "Our poor old father isn't here to protect you anymore. Nobody is here to keep you safe. Your friends, your family, they're all gone. I personally made sure of it." He smiled evilly. His eyes were menacing slits.

Nautilus was spilling over with rage. "One thing I realized about you, Benthos, is that you have great potential. You're smart, brave, strong, charming, and ambitious. But there's one thing you lack—one thing that prevents you from ever being a great leader. You don't have compassion."

Benthos' smile dropped. "Compassion?" he hissed. "Compassion is for the foolish and weak! It's a lie wolves use to deceive the clueless. Nobody is truly good in this world."

Nautilus lashed his tail. "Of course that's what you would think," he retorted. "You've never opened your heart to others—never tried to see the good in anyone."

Benthos smiled coldly at Nautilus. "If I wasn't about to annihilate you in front of the entire empire," he said unpleasantly, "I would tear your fur off here and now. You truly have no idea who I am. Or who I used to be, more fittingly." Benthos angrily adjusted the crown, as if it didn't fit quite properly. "One of the reasons I've despised you so much, Nautilus, is that you remind me of the wolf I used to be as a pup. So trusting. So hopeful. So... insufferable. You always try to see good in everything and everyone. It's a pitiful notion."

"What in Elementa are you blabbing on about?" Nautilus demanded.

Benthos clutched the edge of the throne with his claws. "I used to have a great life, many, many moons ago," he began flatly. "Everything was wonderful. Perfect and carefree. It was the life any naïve pup would want. And then, everything started to go wrong, spiralling out of control before my very eyes. My true parents decided they didn't want me anymore. They had better things to do than bother with me. So, they dumped me at an orphanage, never to be seen again. I tried to stay positive like a *fool*, and made the most out of my situation."

Benthos clenched his jaw. "I tried to find friends, but the other orphans didn't like me," he continued. "They thought I was too big. They were afraid of my shark-like tail and pointy fangs. They made fun of me. Mocked me. Told me I was weird, only because I looked different from them." His fur bristled. "Day after day, night after night, I was teased for things out of my control. When I made gifts for the other pups, they broke my creations in front of my face. If trouble happened at the orphanage, I was always the one blamed, even if I did nothing wrong."

His ears flattened. "Nobody thought highly of me," Benthos continued. "Everyone hated me. I tried everything to show them I was someone good, but nobody cared. For years I rotted away at that orphanage. The other pups were adopted one by one as the days dragged on. But nobody wanted *me*—the big, bad, scary wolf. I tried to show my potential new parents that I was nice, compassionate, and the model pup anyone would want. But nothing I did mattered. All they saw was my scary exterior."

A dangerous glint appeared in Benthos' eyes. "One night, I realized something," he growled. "If nobody liked me for who I was, then I would become someone new. I decided to transform into the monster they all accused me of being." Benthos smirked wickedly. "I was the *first* to start fights with the other pups. I *caused* trouble for everyone around me. I stole, I lied, and I cheated."

"My behaviour was so awful that I was kicked out of the orphanage," Benthos confessed with pride. "It was no fur off my back. I was older, smarter, and bigger than before. There was nothing in the empire that was scarier than me." He barked out a laugh. "I made my presence known to the pack. They were afraid of my very name. I was *given* the respect I always dreamed of having, commanding it to everyone who crossed my path. I was feared, and it was great."

Benthos was silent for a moment. He took off the crown and studied it with narrowed eyes. "I started to get cocky," he grumbled. "Causing mischief at stores and dens didn't excite me anymore. So, I started thinking big. A bit too big. I decided to sneak into the castle to steal this very crown." Benthos glared at Nautilus. "I'm sure you can imagine that my plan backfired rather quickly."

"I was captured by Wave, who was only a rookie guard at the time," Benthos hissed. "She dragged me by the tail to King Delta, demanding that I receive punishment." Benthos' icy gaze softened. "And yet, despite me deserving it, King Delta didn't insult me. He didn't call me names, or yell at me, or accuse me of things I didn't do. King Delta was actually... nice... to me."

"He decided right there and then to adopt me—to raise me as his own son." Benthos stared at nothingness, becoming lost in his thoughts. "His kindness moved me. King Delta changed my heart. Because he was compassionate to me, I decided to give being good another shot. And that's exactly what I did. I became Prince Benthos, the most respectful and well-mannered wolf someone could ever hope to meet."

Benthos' gaze suddenly became livid. "But that all changed when I learned the truth," he snarled. "I overheard King Delta talking with his elderly parents one night, countless moons ago. He was speaking about his pup—his *true* pup. You." Benthos flashed

Nautilus a murderous glare. "I overheard King Delta refer to me as his true son's replacement. I realized in that moment that I was nothing more than a substitute. A backup plan for someone more important and more loved than me!"

Nautilus flinched. "I'm sorry—"

"Silence!" Benthos screamed. "That's when I learned there was no such thing as true compassion. Kindness is simply a lie—an act wolves put on to trick the unsuspecting. I promised myself that I would never be a part of that deceitfulness. Nobody would look at me and see a wolf that I wasn't. Not ever." Pain shimmered in Benthos' yellow eyes. His ears flattened and his tail drooped.

Benthos suddenly lifted himself taller and clasped his front paws together. "Well, that's enough of my monologue for now," he said pleasantly. "Now that you're aware of what you stole from me, I can tear you to pieces in front of the entire empire. Doesn't that sound marvelous?" The wicked, cunning expression returned to Benthos' face.

Nautilus bared his fangs and flexed his claws. "I wish things had been different for you," he told him. "I wish we could have grown up as friends—as brothers, even. But I won't let you harm my empire. Your mind is twisted, and your heart is cold. I won't let you destroy all those innocent wolves; despite how much you think they deserve it."

"Oh, *please*. Save it for the battlefield," Benthos groaned while rolling his eyes. "If I hear you ramble on about how righteous you are for a moment longer, I might just claw you to shreds here and now, you pathetic lump of fur." Benthos glided off the throne like a ghost, his crown shimmering in the dark red light. "Guards!" Benthos abruptly screamed.

Two wolves slithered out of the dark shadows, seeming to materialize out of nowhere. "Yes, King Benthos," they said in haunting unison.

"Round up the entire empire and herd them to the arena," Benthos demanded. "I want every Water Wolf in the ocean to see me destroy my brother. They're going to watch as I ascend permanently to the throne—and they're going to witness the end of King Nautilus forever. I'll show everyone what happens when they defy my leadership."

The guards scurried out of sight.

Benthos' fur appeared black in the blood-red light of the sun. His yellow eyes were wild and ghoulish. "Get ready, Brother!" Benthos screamed. He swam closer, causing a shadow to fall over Nautilus. "This is the beginning of the end!"

CHAPTER 21

The arena rose ominously out of the ocean floor. Nautilus gulped when he swam into its gloomy shadow, feeling chilled to his very bones. The battlefield was surrounded by massive silver pillars that resembled claws and fangs. They circled the edge of the area, enclosing the battling and spectating wolves on all sides.

Nautilus had never seen the arena in person before. Wave hadn't showed it to him during their tour of the empire so many days ago—and with good reason. It was terrifying. Royal wolves only used this battlefield to fight to the very end, settling a disagreement over power with irreversible consequences. King Delta had reluctantly told Nautilus about the arena just so he was aware of its existence, but neither wolf had hoped that Nautilus would actually have to fight in it one day.

And yet, here Nautilus was, moments away from fighting his brother to the death. Why did things have to go so wrong? Couldn't there be a peaceful solution to this problem? This seemed quite extreme in Nautilus' eyes. Perhaps, if he made it out of this alive and secured his place as king, he would discuss finding a better way to resolve royal conflicts with his advisors.

But it was a fleeting thought. Nautilus needed to stay focused on the task in front of him. If he put a single paw out of place, he'd be a goner. The empire would be at his brother's mercy, with nobody to stand in his way. Nautilus couldn't afford to mess this up.

He glanced at his brother, who soundlessly glided beside him like a dangerous predator. Benthos' ears were flattened. His yellow eyes were as hard as diamonds, while his jaw was clenched. The royal crown glimmered on top of Benthos' head, radiating tremendous power.

Nautilus wanted to reason with his brother, but he knew that it would be a waste of breath. There was no reasoning with Benthos. He was broken beyond repair, so misguided that he couldn't tell the difference between right and wrong. Nautilus wished he could help Benthos heal, but the scars his brother carried were unrepairable. Benthos had left Nautilus no other choice but to fight. It was the only way to end their royal rivalry—forever.

The arena was filled to the brim with nervous wolves as Nautilus and Benthos swam to the middle of the battlefield. Guards hovered in the water above the spectators, ensuring they wouldn't flee the arena. Every Water Wolf in the ocean was forced to watch this momentous clash on Benthos' orders.

Are they all going to watch me die? Nautilus wondered nervously. It felt like spiders were scurrying through his fur. His heart was beating so fast that he thought it would burst out of his chest.

As Nautilus swam weakly to the middle of the battlefield, his surroundings began to blur in and out of focus. It felt like the ocean was swaying and spinning. Nautilus' heartbeat became quicker, and quicker, and even quicker than before. Just before Nautilus fainted from fear—

"You can do this King Nautilus!" came a sudden cheer from the crowd.

"We believe in you King Nautilus!" someone else shouted.

"All hail King Nautilus!" exclaimed another.

The entire arena began to roar with support, so loudly that their voices could be heard from above the waves. "King Nautilus! King Nautilus! King Nautilus!" Every Water Wolf started to cheer his name, over and over again, with such emotion that Nautilus nearly cried out with joy. Even the guards, who were being forced to obey Benthos, joined in.

The pack believed in him. They wanted *him* to be their leader. After everything that happened, after so much heartache and pain, Nautilus was seen as a rightful king in their eyes. It caused an indescribable feeling of happiness, one that Nautilus would never, ever forget.

Benthos suddenly slashed the side of Nautilus' head. The rage on his face was nightmarish. "This is the wolf you want as king?!" Benthos screamed to the pack. "Prepare to watch him die!" Benthos rushed at Nautilus with outstretched claws.

Nautilus dodged to the side—but he wasn't fast enough. Benthos ruthlessly tore his claws across Nautilus' chest. Before Nautilus could recover, Benthos violently slammed him against the ocean floor, then sunk his fangs into his neck.

Nautilus let out a howl of pain. He thrashed and kicked, but couldn't free himself from Benthos' grasp. The water began to turn red. *I can't die now!* Nautilus thought fearfully. *All these wolves—they're counting on me! I need to fight back! I have to protect them!* Nautilus twisted around and managed to dig his fangs into Benthos' shoulder, who reared back with a hiss of rage.

Benthos' surprise quickly faded. He lashed out again, aiming to deliver a devastating blow, then abruptly recoiled with a yell of pain. Nautilus' bite had been more effective than he'd first realized. Benthos could barely move his forearm.

Nautilus lifted off the sea floor, growling dangerously. He immediately clawed Benthos with all his strength, delivering a nasty wound. "That was for Ember!" Nautilus shouted angrily. He swiped again. "That was for Aurora!" He sliced Benthos' ear. "That was for all the trouble you caused Wave, my father, and all my packmates!" Nautilus knocked into Benthos and slammed him against the ocean floor. "And that was for everything you did to me!"

Benthos' body shook with pain. He tried to look fierce as he glared up at Nautilus, but anguish and shock were written all over his face. Benthos attempted to stumble to his paws, but immediately collapsed again. Nautilus couldn't believe it. Had he won? It just seemed... too easy.

"King Nautilus!" the arena howled. Their voices echoed through the ocean. "King Nautilus!"

Nautilus moved away from Benthos, his concerns forgotten. He stared at his empire in awe, releasing a shuddering breath of relief.

Suddenly, Benthos exploded to Nautilus and barrelled into him. The two brothers wildly tumbled up and down, over and over again. Benthos quickly managed to overpower Nautilus. He pinned him to the ocean floor, growling lividly. "Say goodbye, Brother," Benthos hissed through clenched teeth. He opened his muzzle with a thunderous snarl, prepared to dig his fangs into Nautilus' throat.

Nautilus slammed his eyes shut.

There was a terrible roar of fury, and Benthos' weight was lifted off Nautilus. What in Elementa just happened?! Nautilus scrambled to his paws. He gasped. Three guards were dragging Benthos away from Nautilus, struggling to contain the wild wolf. Benthos screamed and kicked and thrashed, doing everything he could to break free from the guards. "RELEASE ME!" Benthos screeched. "Nautilus was mine! I was about to win!"

"It's clear to everyone that King Nautilus is our rightful ruler," one of the guards snarled. "He doesn't need to win a fight to prove that. Benthos, your reign of fear is over!" Benthos released a scream of pure rage. Bubbles exploded out of his mouth. The anger in his eyes was horrifying. Nautilus shuddered.

It took the help of two extra guards to contain Benthos. They pressed him against the ocean floor. Nautilus, seeing that Benthos was no longer a threat, cautiously swam closer to his brother. As he did, a murderous glint appeared in Benthos' yellow eyes. "Don't think this is over," he spat at Nautilus, struggling to breathe because of the weight on top of him. "I know you. You're weak. Soft. Too afraid of what it takes to be powerful."

"Oh, would you shut your muzzle already?" Nautilus growled. "Let me guess. You think that I need to kill you to be strong. Is that right?"

Benthos bared his pointy fangs. "Of course that's right," he snarled. "What kind of fool keeps their enemies alive? You can lock me in the darkest dungeon known to Elementa, but I'll still find you. Nautilus, while I'm alive, you won't ever be safe from me. One way or another, I'll manage to reach you, and you'll be dead."

Nautilus extended a paw and picked up the crown, which had fallen off Benthos' head during the fight. He held it close to his heart. "That's all fine and good," Nautilus retorted. "But you fail to realize one crucial thing, Benthos. I'm not afraid of you anymore. You can scheme and threaten me all you want. It doesn't matter. Look around you! The entire pack supports me—and I support them. How can I fail when all these wolves have my back? There's no way that the Water Pack will fall. Not when each of us are working together as one."

Hearing his words, the arena erupted with cheer, voicing their support for Nautilus. Benthos' eyes widened with bewilderment.

"Violence doesn't always have to be the answer," Nautilus continued. He placed the crown on his head, glad to be reunited with it at last. "A true leader doesn't need to scare their followers to earn loyalty and respect. Benthos, I said it before, and I'll say it again. You could have been great."

Nautilus sighed. "I understand how much you've been hurt in life. You and I weren't so different once. I know what it's like to shut out the world and to harden your heart. It's scary to open yourself up to others, knowing how easily you can be hurt. But there's no greater reward than finding true friends, and a real place to call home."

"You're insufferable," Benthos snarled in a low, dangerous voice. "You self-righteous, goody-four-paw, tail biting fool. I should have torn you to bits when I had the chance. If only Wave hadn't stopped me that day, when you and I met for the second time. I would've been king by now. The entire ocean would've been mine to command." Greed sparkled in his eyes.

Nautilus felt disgusted. "Let him stand," he ordered the guards. "I can't allow him to stay in our empire for a moment longer." Nautilus stared directly into Benthos' eyes as he lifted himself. "Get out. Leave the pack forever, never to return. You've proven that you don't belong among us."

Benthos let out a rough bark of a laugh. "Oh, I don't belong?!" he sneered. Nautilus' eyes widened, immediately knowing where this was going. "How can you possibly say that, you abomination hybrid?!"

The pack gasped. Nautilus felt a sudden sensation of vertigo, like he was falling backward. *My secret,* he thought in sheer horror. *No!*

Benthos was livid as he glared at the Water Wolves. A few guards tried to drag him out of the arena, but Benthos dodged them with a threatening hiss. He faced the crowd. "Don't you fools realize that *I'm* the best choice for king?" he demanded. "Who would you rather be led by? Me, or this half Fire Wolf monstrosity?"

There was a terrible, deafening silence for a moment. Then—

"You're the monstrosity!" someone in the crowd hollered.

"It doesn't matter who King Nautilus is!" another wolf screamed. "He's proven his goodness!"

Tears fell from Nautilus' eyes before he could help it. He sobbed with happiness—unable to believe that he was finally being accepted for who he was. As the crowd continued to cry out with loyalty for their new king, Benthos' rage continued to grow. "If I can't get a happy ending," he snarled, "Then neither can Nautilus!"

With a furious scream, Benthos rushed at Nautilus, refusing to give up when he was clearly defeated. Benthos barely managed to travel a few tail lengths before being intercepted by the guards. They dragged him out of the arena, eager to banish him from the empire forever.

"I'll find you!" Benthos screeched at Nautilus. "I'll get my claws on you. You'll be dead! I'll make you regret the day you were born! You'll wish that you never even looked at the ocean! You hear me?! This isn't over! I'll destroy you. I'll destroy you all!"

Rolling her eyes, a guard plucked a long tendril of seaweed from the ocean floor and used it to wrap Benthos' snout shut. With a muffled shriek of protest, Benthos was whisked out of sight. Nautilus watched him go with a sigh of relief.

Despite Benthos' threats, Nautilus knew in his heart that he wouldn't be seeing his brother again. Benthos was a smart wolf. He wouldn't dare start another a fight when he had no chance of winning.

Nautilus lifted his head to the sky. It felt like a weight had been lifted off of his shoulders. *I won,* he thought. *Our royal rivalry is finally over. I'm the new king of the Water Pack Empire... and it feels awesome.*

"All hail King Nautilus!" the pack cheered joyously. "All hail our true king!"

EPILOGUE

A cool current flowed around Nautilus' pelt. He drew in a deep breath, his gills fluttering. For the first time in what seemed like forever, Nautilus felt at peace—and so did the Water Pack Empire. A busy week had passed, and during that time, they had worked hard to rebuild the aquatic kingdom.

The Royal Memorial, which was torn down by Benthos, had been reconstructed with even more beauty than before.

All of Benthos' prisoners, including Wave, had been freed.

And, to Nautilus' delight, the Water Pack Empire was slowly being introduced to the Sky Pack Kingdom. Unity across Elementa was closer than ever before, thanks to Nautilus.

Water Wolves cheerily greeted their king as he swam passed them. Nautilus returned their bright smiles. However, despite his calm outward appearance, something was troubling him. Everything was finally perfect in Nautilus' life—all expect for one glaring issue.

Nautilus sighed with relief when he finally swam outside of the empire's borders. The vast ocean ahead of him was still and quiet. It felt nice to be alone with his thoughts—to have no wolves asking him for advice or orders. Nautilus had spent most of his life as a lone wolf, after all. It was still strange to be the leader of an entire pack. Nautilus wasn't sure if he would ever get used to it.

Nautilus silently glided through the ocean, allowing himself to become lost in his own mindscape. He wasn't concerned about anyone attacking him. Not like before. Benthos was clearly long gone. He hadn't been spotted since his banishment after the Battle of Power. Perhaps Benthos had abandoned the ocean altogether, or fled Elementa entirely. There were rumours of lands far beyond their continent. It was possible that Benthos had decided to go someplace far away from the known packs.

As for Benthos' followers, Nautilus swiftly discovered and fairly punished them for their crimes. Luckily, there had only been a few loyalists, and most were only guilty of minor offenses.

The worst of Benthos' supporters was named Coral, who happened to be the wolf that attacked Nautilus near Emora Island all those moons ago. Coral carried a suspicious scorch mark on her shoulder, and it didn't take long for Nautilus to realize that she was the wolf he burned while in his Fire Wolf form. Nautilus was glad to finally solve the mystery of who ambushed him that day.

No. Benthos and his followers weren't what bothered Nautilus right now.

Grimacing, Nautilus swam faster through the ocean, his heart aching to see the truth. A single thought had been swirling through his mind without ceasing. Nautilus decided it was time to get some answers... even if they weren't the answers he was hoping for.

Before long, Nautilus reached the shore of Emora Island. Nautilus hesitated below the waves for a few moments, feeling nervous. Then, with a deep breath, he lifted himself out of the water and moved to dry land. The exotic jungle trees swayed in the billowing breeze, while macaws screeched and glided overhead. Nautilus slowly walked deeper into the island, the white sand squelching beneath his paws.

As he neared the meadow where Aurora and Ember used to camp, the faint smell of smoke hit his nose. Nautilus stepped into the burnt clearing with hesitant pawsteps.

His heart sunk.

The treehouse that his friends built was nothing more than a pile of ash. All their hard work was destroyed, beyond repair, and nothing more than a distant memory. The sight was enough to make Nautilus whimper. He sat down, lowering his head with a sigh. A part of him had hoped that, somehow,

Aurora and Ember would've found their way back here. Nautilus had desperately dreamed of a happy reunion between him and his friends—that everything would magically return to how it was.

But it had been foolish to dream.

Aurora and Ember were gone, and Nautilus could only begin to guess where. Forcing himself to be strong, he rose to his paws. Nautilus lingered for a brief moment, gazing solemnly at the wreckage. He then turned around and walked back to the ocean, imagining the faces of his friends. *I hope you guys are safe out there,* he thought. *Wherever you are...*

***

Far across the ocean, trapped behind obsidian bars, was Ember. He pawed frantically at the rods, his heart racing. *Time is running out,* he thought. *I need to get out of here.* He desperately tugged at the door of his cage, but couldn't make it budge. Fear oozed through his veins—he began to feel dizzy. All the heat from the lava rivers, and the smoke that billowed through the air, made him shudder.

A snarl suddenly cut through the silence. The guard turned her head to angrily scowl at her prisoner. Her patience had finally run out. "Would you *please* stop struggling?" she demanded. "Why can't you be quiet like a normal prisoner?"

"Flare," Ember pleaded, clutching the bars with his paws. "Listen to me. You're in as much danger as I am. King Inferno is going to—"

"Silence!" Flare hissed.

"King Inferno is going to kill you right alongside me, once he finds out you lost Nautilus and Aurora," Ember pressed. "You're not a fool, Sister. You know that your life is in danger."

Flare looked away, growling. Although she said nothing, Ember could sense her fear. *This is the moment I've been waiting for,* he realized. *I can't let this opportunity slip through my claws.* "You and I have always been the smartest of our siblings," Ember continued. "I see you as an equal, Flare, and I know that the two of us can find a way out of this. You and I don't have to die today. We can fight back against King Inferno—together."

Flare turned to look at Ember. To his surprise, there wasn't rage in her eyes. She only looked horrified. "How can you be certain?" Flare asked, trying in vain to keep her voice steady. "Father has raised us to fear him. He's shown us what happens to wolves who defy him more times than I can count. There's no hope for us."

Ember lashed his tail. "Yes there is," he said stubbornly. "Come on, Flare. I know you. You aren't a coward. Where's your fighting spirit? Don't tell me you've lost your nerve so easily." Ember moved closer to the edge of the cage. "We can do this, Sister. There's still time to figure out a plan."

"Perhaps," Flare said cautiously. "Father won't be back from his raid on the Earth Pack until tonight." She frowned, thinking carefully. "Why don't we sneak out of the Fire Pack Dominion now, before he returns? We'll be halfway across Elementa by the time Father realizes we're gone."

Ember shook his head. "He'll find us," he said nervously. "No matter where we run, or how much we hide, King Inferno will catch us. Trust me. I know from experience that a wolf is never truly free of him."

Flare gulped, her ears flattening. "So what chance do we have?" she asked.

Ember gazed past his sister to stare at the volcanic wasteland beyond. His paws curled into trembling fists. "I have an idea," Ember said shakily. "It's risky, but it might just work. If we pull it off the way I'm imagining, you and I will never know fear again."

Flare was silent for a painfully long moment, considering every word Ember said. He found himself holding his breath. Would Flare cooperate with Ember? If she refused to be a part of his plan, then there would be no hope for either sibling. *Come on,* Ember thought. *Don't give up on me now. We need each other!*

"Fine," Flare eventually said. "I'll hear what you have to say."

Ember let out a sigh of relief. "Thank you," he huffed. "Okay. Here's the plan..."

**

Meanwhile, Aurora struggled to fly through the violent winds of a storm. Her massive wings shook uncontrollably in the turbulence, and her white fur lashed wildly. Rain painfully smacked against Aurora's pelt, but she refused to slow down. Her green eyes were narrowed in determination.

Those Fire Wolves are going to regret laying a single claw on my friends! Aurora thought fiercely. *I'll make them pay for what they did! Nobody hurts my friends and gets away with it.* The chains that were tightly wrapped around Aurora's muzzle only added to her rage. Thunder roared through the dark sky. Lightning flashed through the clouds in the distance, while wind shrieked in her ears. The ferocious weather matched Aurora's mood perfectly.

She suddenly swooped, recognizing the landscape down below. *Finally,* she thought. *I'm almost there.* Aurora glided close to the ground, keeping her eyes sharp for what she was desperately looking for. After a few minutes of patrolling the area, Aurora spotted it.

The Howl Dome—the arena located right at the heart of the Earth Pack City. Aurora had reached her destination at last.

She tucked in her wings, allowing herself to plummet to the ground. Aurora wasn't concerned about being spotted by potentially hostile Earth Wolves. Nobody other than Aurora was foolish enough to be outside in a storm like this.

Sodden and exhausted, the Sky Wolf landed with a thud in the centre of the arena. It was dark inside, and eerily silent. Aurora barely recognized the Howl Dome. Everything had been so chaotic when she had last been here. It was strange to see it so peaceful.

Aurora nervously smiled at the battlefield. *Oh, I recognize that spot over there,* she thought. *That's where Sandstorm knocked me out cold, giving me my scar.* Aurora turned her head to look at the many rows of seats in the distance. *And that's where I was being dragged down by the crowd to fight Sandstorm. I have such fantastic memories of this place,* Aurora thought sarcastically.

She gave her pelt a shake, causing droplets of water to fly in every direction. *I need to stay focused,* Aurora reminded herself. *Who knows what trouble Nautilus and Ember are facing right now. My friends are counting on me.*

Aurora started to walk around the arena, scanning the area for Sandstorm. She was the only wolf Aurora could turn to for help. Sandstorm was strong, brave, and always ready for a fight. But would the Earth Wolf be willing to help Aurora again?

I can't be sure until I ask her, she thought. *That's easier said than done, though. It doesn't look like Sandstorm is here.* Aurora felt a surge of frustration. *I'll have to wait in the arena until she shows up. It's the only choice I have. I don't know where Sandstorm lives, and it's too dangerous to wander around the Earth Pack looking for her.*

With a sigh of frustration, Aurora made her way to the stone seats, preparing to hide until Sandstorm appeared.

Without warning, something emerged from the shadows behind Aurora. A dark shape suddenly pounced on the Sky Wolf and wrestled her to the ground. With a fierce growl, Aurora lashed a paw in the direction of her attacker, but the wolf skillfully dodged the blow. Aurora was about to lash out again—but stopped herself. Her green eyes widened.

It was Sandstorm!

Recognition filled the Earth Wolf's amber eyes. "Ugh. It's you," she growled while stepping away from Aurora. "What in Elementa are you doing, sneaking around inside my arena?"

Sandstorm suddenly spotted the chains on Aurora's snout. "For the moon's sake!" she hissed. "Don't tell me that you need my help *again*!"

Aurora rose to her paws and shook the dirt off her pelt. She met Sandstorm's gaze and nodded.

Sandstorm rolled her eyes. "What have the three of you gotten yourselves into this time?" she snapped.

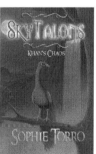

Draven the outcast thief and Sora the runaway princess must defy the odds and put a stop to the perilous eternal day. Will the two unlikely heroes manage to save their home?

ABOUT THE AUTHOR

Sophie Torro is a teen author. In 2019, at the age of 15, she published the first novel in the *SkyTalons* series. It has quickly gained worldwide praise and popularity. The following novels in the *SkyTalons* series were published shortly afterward, along with her new series, *Griffin Quest* and *The Wolves of Elementa*. Sophie has also written and illustrated the educational *Q&A Kids* series. Sophie lives in Canada, where she works on her future novels and other exciting projects.

2·23

Made in the USA
Columbia, SC
16 November 2022

71360924R00148